UNCLE SHAWN AND BILL

UNCLE SHAWN AND BILL

AND THE ALMOST ENTIRELY
UNPLANNED ADVENTURE

WORRIED
LLAMA
↙

A. L. KENNEDY
ILLUSTRATED BY GEMMA CORRELL

WALKER
BOOKS

First published 2017 by Walker Books Ltd
87 Vauxhall Walk, London SE11 5HJ

This edition published 2018

2 4 6 8 10 9 7 5 3 1

Text © 2017 A. L. Kennedy • Illustrations © 2017 Gemma Correll

The right of A. L. Kennedy and Gemma Correll to be identified as author
and illustrator respectively of this work has been asserted by them in
accordance with the Copyright, Designs and Patents Act 1988

This book has been typeset in Sabon and Gemma Correll Regular

Printed and bound by CPI Group (UK) Ltd, Croydon CR0 4YY

British Library Cataloguing in Publication Data: a catalogue
record for this book is available from the British Library

ISBN 978-1-4063-7833-7

www.walker.co.uk

MIX
Paper from
responsible sources
FSC® C020471

MEANIES

For Honor and Xavier

With Thanks

HEROIC BADGER

SECTION ONE

*In which a brave and handsome young badger
called Bill meets two extremely dreadful sisters
and begins an adventure he may not survive. He
also has a sore ear and remembers that he doesn't
like shorts, especially when he is wearing them.*

Badger Bill was having a very bad evening, maybe
the worst of his whole life. He was stuck inside
a bag. It was an extremely scratchy and horrible
bag and it smelled as if someone who was also a
badger had been crying inside it a few days ear-
lier and then maybe after that had been sick. Bill
was small and young but very clever, and he was

BILL

MOUTH ORGAN →

SNOUT WITH HIGHLY DEVELOPED SENSE OF SMELL →

STUBBY (BUT SHAPELY) ← LEGS

able to guess that whoever had snatched him up when he wasn't expecting it and put him in the bag was now *carrying him somewhere*. He was being bounced and banged about with no care at all, so whoever was carrying him horribly in the horrible sack was probably a horrible person. Badgers have a highly developed sense of smell and he could tell just in one sniff that whoever was carrying him had a heart full of nails and sand and nastiness.

Bill guessed he was balanced over the horrible person's shoulder. Every now and then what he thought might be their elbow banged him hard in the back of his neck. And he was definitely upside down. This all suggested that the horrible person and the horrible bag were heading for somewhere that would also turn out to be horrible. This made Bill worried. It would make anyone worried – even if they were clever and brave. Meanwhile, the big, horrible feet of the big, horrible person pounded onwards.

Bill's whiskers were all bent, his ears were dented and he felt miserable and bruised and very puzzled. "But I was just out for a stroll," he thought to himself. "I was going to pick some sage and make tea with it when I got home. Only then I turned left instead of right and I got distracted by those squirrels talking about having seen some llamas. Everyone knows there aren't any llamas anywhere near here. Llamas come from South

America and we're in Scotland. And after I had explained this for the eighth time – squirrels are so stupid – I couldn't quite remember where I wanted to go and I ... I sort of got lost..."

Bill was embarrassed that he'd got lost, because he had always wanted to be a famous explorer when he was older. There were many great badger explorers – Horatio Badger, who canoed round the Himalayas, for example; or Matilda Badger, who ran with the buffalo on the Great Plains of America until she died of excitement at the age of 87.

Bill was ashamed. "I got a little bit lost and then I thought I saw a weasel looking nastily at me from under a bush. It was just a weaselly shadow, but I ran away from it and that made me get *really* lost." Which is often what happens when we're tired and aren't really sure where we are and then get scared as well. "And now I'm thirsty and lonely and whoever is carrying me smells of being unkind and I already know

WEASELLY SHADOW →

↗ SCARED (but brave) BADGER

they're unkind because they *put me in a bag.*
Without asking. All I want to do is go home and
sit in my little badger rocking chair and play my
mouth organ until I feel happier, and then go to
bed. And maybe have a hot chocolate and a let-
tuce sandwich first. And a biscuit. And then an
apple." He was a resourceful badger, but he felt
much smaller than usual, and wobbly. "But I'm
not at home. I'm in a bag! Why would anybody
want a bag of badger?"

Before he could be puzzled any more he suddenly smelled the smell of someone else horrible nearby and felt himself being swung downwards, shaken roughly and tipped out of the bag onto a cold stone floor. He landed all in a heap. "Ow!" he squealed. Then he tried to make himself sound more courageous by shouting, in as deep a voice as he could manage, "What are you doing with me? You, you..."

Only then he stopped speaking, because standing over him were two of the hugest human beings he had ever seen. They were probably ladies, but they were each as wide as a wardrobe and seemed almost as high as a bus. Their hands were grubby and leathery and bigger than Bill's head. Both women seemed to have no necks, just as if someone had dumped their huge meaty faces straight down onto the collars of their dirty pink cardigans. Or maybe their necks didn't like them and had run away and left them. The humans

PROBABLY LADIES

VERY NASTY HAT

NO NECKS

ETHEL   MAUDE

had eyes that were tiny and cross-looking and the colour of bad-flavoured boiled sweets, and they were studying Badger Bill. He didn't enjoy being studied. It made him feel like homework, or arithmetic. Or dinner.

13

The woman with the meatiest head was wearing a yellow knitted hat with a purple flower in it, which didn't suit her. It wouldn't have suited anyone. She peered at Bill and growled, "Well, he's got spirit. Where did you catch him, Sister Maude, my pet?" Her voice sounded like dropping something ugly down a well.

Sister Maude hissed, "Found him wandering about near the river, Sssissster Ethel, my ssssweet. He's not very big though, isss he?"

Badger Bill thought that not many creatures would seem remotely big near either Ethel or Maude – apart from maybe a very inflatable hippo. Even so, he tried to stand up straight and bristle out his fur. "I'm big for my age. Everyone says so."

"Oooh." Maude gave an extremely unpleasant hoot, as if she'd recently swallowed an owl alive, which Badger Bill suspected might be likely. "It can talk. That'sss unusssual in a badger." She didn't know that many of the animals she had met, poked with sticks, pinched and shouted at during her long and spiteful life could have talked to her if they'd wanted to. The thing was that none of them *had* wanted to. "We should take advantage of that and make him give resssitationsss. Or, then again – we could make *piesss*."

Ethel nodded nastily and tweaked Bill's cheek between her great big dirty finger and her great big dirty thumb. "Indeed, Sister Maude. First we have the fight to prepare for. And afterwards … *pies*."

OWL PIE   DORMOUSE PIE

FOX PIE   BADGER PIE?!

Bill didn't like the way Ethel had winked at him when she'd said pies. Bill also really hoped that when they talked about a fight they meant that Ethel and Maude were going to fight each other. He definitely didn't want them to fight *him*. He didn't want to fight anyone – he was a very peace-ful badger.

Then Maude said something else worrying: "Yesss, I think the red shortsss will fit him." Bill hated shorts. They made his legs look stumpy.

Ethel kept staring at Bill with her eyes that were like old, bad eggs. It looked like she might be thinking and that thinking hurt her head, because it didn't happen often. Then she spoke. "The red shorts with the white stripe and the red boots. No gloves, of course…" Ethel giggled with the sound of plumbing gone horribly wrong and Bill knew that seeming to have stumpy legs was going to be the least of his problems.

Bill shuddered. "Ahm, you … er … lovely

ladies wouldn't be suggesting that I in any way should be involved in fisticuffs, would you? Me, myself, personally? Because I'm not a fighting kind of badger. I don't even like shouting."

FIGHTING BADGER   PEACEFUL BADGER

MEAN
GENTLE
SNARLY
ANGRY
QUIET
DOES NOT WEAR RED SHORTS

Ethel and Maude grinned at him with their thick, greasy, left-over-sausage kind of lips. This made his whole tummy go cold.

"No, honestly. I'm allergic to shorts. And why no gloves, by the way? What if my hands get chilly, or I bang my knuckles against something hard?" Badger Bill swallowed and it felt as if he had a bit of unhappy sandwich stuck in his throat.

Ethel sucked in air between her long, brown teeth. "Of course you'll be good at fighting, dearie. Battling Badger Bob – that's you."

"Bill. My name's Bill," corrected Badger Bill. "William J. Badger, actually, if I'm filling out a form or something important. The J is for January, because that's when it's my birthday." The two women didn't look as if they wanted to know when his birthday was. And he suspected that they wouldn't be giving him a present – not even a single tiny present between the two of them.

Ethel hit one of his soft, furry badger ears with the back of her hand. This stung him and made his head go twirly. "You'll be called Battling Badger Bob from now on, dearie, and don't you forget it."

Maude nodded. "The fight'sss on Sssaturday. Aren't you the lucky badger, then?"

Bill didn't feel lucky at all. This was Thursday night, which meant that he only had Friday left … and then it would be bad, bad, bad Saturday.

And he'd always liked Saturdays before this, so he thought it was a shame.

Maude leaned close to Bill while she spoke. His whiskers twitched with nerves and his sensitive nose tried to ignore her snaky breath, which smelled like drains and very, very old sardines. "Come along now," she said, and she picked him up by his back legs and started to carry him off upside down, his head swinging about beside her knees. "Time for bed. You'll need your ressst. Don't worry – we'll help you with your training."

Badger Bill felt the blood rushing to his ears – especially the stinging one – and tried not to let his nose brush against the stained hem of Maude's lime-green corduroy skirt. "Madam, this is

undignified! I could just walk! Please. This is all a mistake!" he shouted up at her.

But she only said, "*Madam*! *Madam*, indeed... Who doesss he think he isss, the Archbishop of Canterbury?" And she chuckled, which produced a noise like wet hens running into each other. And then she swung him back and forth a little bit harder.

Badger Bill thought of all the times in his life when he had sat up at night and worried himself about horrifying things that had never happened. Now he wished that he had saved his energy for today, when something horrifying really *was* happening and he didn't know what to do. He was a shy badger and hadn't made many friends at school. Since then he had kept himself to himself. Bill realized this meant that nobody would miss him, or notice that he'd gone – not even if he never, never, never came back home. He needed rescuing, but he was the only person who knew it. Bill tried not to cry, because he guessed that making handsome young badgers cry was one of Maude's favourite hobbies.

MAUDE'S FAVOURITE HOBBIES

MAKING HANDSOME YOUNG BADGERS CRY

POKING WEASELS WITH STICKS

BULLYING BUNNIES

For the first time ever, Badger Bill realized that he felt lonely in each of his paws and every one of his whiskers and all the way into his heart, which was a good heart and full of good things. He folded his paws around his long badger nose and held tight and wished that he knew what to do and that someone would help him.

SISKIN
HAVING FUN

SECTION TWO

In which we meet some unusual weather and
four llamas who are already very sad and about
to get much sadder. We also learn a little about
the weather, llamas and poems about socks.

Meanwhile, on the dark side of an incredibly rainy hill, four llamas were trying to find shelter. It was only raining on their hill and not on anywhere else. In fact, it seemed only to be raining right where they were standing. If they ran extremely fast, they could almost get out from under their personal rain-cloud, so that water drops might stop falling on the tips of their noses for a few

strides. But then the weather would catch up with them again when they got tired and slowed down. They were drenched all the time and underneath their fur their skins had gone all wrinkly, as if they'd been in the bath too long.

They could see that all around them the countryside was dry and sunny and flowers were nodding in light breezes. Several small greenish-yellowish birds called siskins were playing tig in and out of the warm tree-branches and wearing sunglasses, because it was so bright. If the llamas had been closer to the siskins, they would even have overheard the little birds talking about getting some ice cream later, before they got too

ICE CREAM

GOOD → TIMES

hot. Then again, if the llamas had been closer to the siskins, the siskins would have been underneath the rain-cloud and wet and depressed.

Above the llamas it wasn't just raining now, it was pouring, and there might even be sleet and snow on the way. Their patch of sky was miserable and they were, too.

Brian Llama sneezed. Then he shook his head and his shoulders, which made a long swirl of water come out of his coat and hit the others. "Oh," he said, "my sore hoof aches."

Guinevere Llama sniffed. "It was a terrible idea to come here. All the way from Peru, for this. You're an idiot."

"Yes, he is an idiot," agreed Ginalolobrigida Llama. "But it did say in the advertisement that Scotland was always sunny and hot and that the McGloone Farm was the most marvellous farm anywhere on earth and that we would have as much lemonade as we could drink and hammocks

to sleep in. And we believed it, so we are all idiots."
Ginalolobrigida Llama didn't ever like to think she
had done anything wrong. "But Brian is the biggest
idiot." Saying that made her feel a little bit better.

They had all read the very lovely advertisement
in *The Lima Llama Informer* which had shown
them glossy photographs and used lots of long and
impressive words. It had invited adventurous llamas to submit short poems about why socks were
useful. The four llamas who wrote the best poems
were promised a free holiday at what had seemed
to be the wonderful McGloone Farm in Scotland.
By now the llamas were pretty sure that the photographs had been of some other farm and that the
holiday was going to last for ever and be dreadful.

"That advertisement was a lie." Brian sneezed
again. "The McGloone Farm isn't a nice farm
and Farmer McGloone isn't a nice man and his
McGloone wife isn't a nice wife and his five
McGloone children are the nastiest children I've

THE WORLD-FAMOUS
McGloone Llama Paradise

ALL LLAMAS WELCOME
TO SUNNY SCOTLAND!

TOP QUALITY HAMMOCKS
24 HOUR BALLET INSTRUCTION
<u>NO</u> POKING WITH STICKS

Accept no inferior paradises!

CHOOSE McGLOONE'S McGLORIOUS McGETAWAY

ever met. And his McGloone sisters are worse
than that. They pick their noses and then wipe
their fingers in my ears."

The sisters, Maude and Ethel, who were being
so nasty to Bill were, of course, the McGloone
sisters. They were McGloones so horrifying and
grumpy that even the other McGloones didn't
want them around and they had to live in their
own cottage full of failed knitting and cat bones

and other terrible things. Of course, the sisters said they wouldn't dream of living in the main farmhouse, because of how ugly, noisy and unbearable the rest of the McGloones were. The only thing all the McGloones could really agree on was how much fun it was to be cruel to everyone they met. Or everyone they tricked into visiting, or kidnapped and shoved into bags.

Back in the field – out of sight of both the cottage and the farmhouse – Carlos Llama sighed. "Farmer McGloone has ruined my wool."

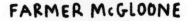

"He's ruined all of our wool!" Brian couldn't help shouting because he was so fed up with Farmer McGloone, and Mrs Myrtle McGloone – Farmer McGloone's wife – coming by with

FARMER McGLOONE

28

the big, clanky shears and taking as much llama wool as they could from the llamas, until they were nearly bald and terribly cold.

MYRTLE McGLOONE

Brian Llama had had a particularly silky chocolate coat and Carlos and Guinevere had had very splendid chocolate and cream and fawn coats and Ginalolobrigida Llama had had a delightful pinky cream coat. They had been four of the proudest and handsomest and loveliest llamas in Peru. In fact, many of the other Peruvian llamas had been quite glad when they left, because being so wonderful had sometimes made the four of them boastful, and boring – as all boastful people are. Brian, Guinevere, Carlos and Ginalolobrigida Llama had thought all the llamas who came to wave them off when they got on the boat to sail away across the ocean were being friendly. In fact, quite a lot of them were actually there to make sure that they really did go away. Of course, our four llama chums were not boastful now. They would probably never boast again – or not until they felt better and were dry. There are few things sadder than a soaked and patchy llama.

Brian snuffed and licked his poorly hoof. "Farmer McGloone promised us luxury llama sheds to sleep in and then we just got that rotten old tent that fell to bits the first night we arrived."

"That was because you sneezed in it," said Ginalolobrigida Llama.

"If it fell apart just because I sneezed, then it wasn't a good tent!" shouted Brian. "I hate it here."

In the entire history of llamas there had never been four llamas who were more depressed, or more disappointed. 🐾

BORED RABBIT

SECTION THREE

In which we meet the great and wonderful and peculiar man who is Uncle Shawn. Even though he is unusual and wears no socks, without Uncle Shawn we're all in trouble. So here he is.

Meanwhile, an extremely tall and quite thin person called Uncle Shawn was sitting near the river. His lanky arms were folded round his gangly, big legs at around about the height of his bony, big knees, which were tucked up under his chin. He was wearing no socks because he had given half his last pair to a young squirrel who wanted to play at camping and use it as a sleeping bag. The squirrel had never brought it back. Uncle Shawn knew that wearing just one sock would have made him lopsided – so he wasn't wearing any. His trousers had very many holes and tears in them, which he didn't sew up because he thought they made him look as if he had adventures. And there was a mother mole dozing in one of his trouser pockets. His other pocket was full of toasted cheese fingers, in case he got hungry. His eyes were blue as two pieces of sky on a good Bank Holiday Monday by the sea with extra crisps and ice cream. If you looked at him quickly, you could tell he was someone very fond of fun, and if you looked at him more carefully, you could tell that he was much more clever than he often pretended to be. And on Uncle Shawn's head was Uncle Shawn's gingery-browny hair, which stood up in spikes and waves and knots.

SQUIRREL USING
A SOCK AS A
SLEEPING BAG

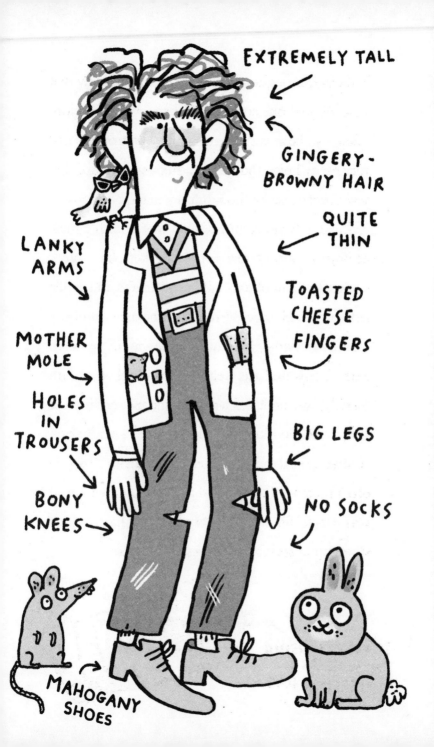

And if you looked at Uncle Shawn really, really carefully – which is how to find out about anyone properly – you would see that if you were in trouble, he was exactly the right man to help you. He was maybe one of the kindest and best humans in the world. But he didn't know that and so he was sometimes a little sad.

Uncle Shawn had no friends he could really talk to at the moment, except for a mainly very serious horse called Paul, who was no good at jokes. And Paul was only visiting him and usually lived in Wales. Uncle Shawn had always wanted lots of friends to enjoy jokes with him, and maybe singing and dancing and cakes and things.

PAUL →

(NO GOOD AT JOKES)

Uncle Shawn whistled, "Tootle-ootle-tooo," and tried speaking to the rabbit that was resting near him in the sun: "What do you get if you sit under a cow?"

The rabbit blinked and nibbled some grass.

The man tried again. "All right then. What's brown and sticky?"

The rabbit blinked once more and then closed its eyes as if it was going to doze off.

"Oh, dear. You're no good at jokes, are you?" Uncle Shawn sighed unhappily. "What did the mother brush say to the baby brush?"

The rabbit started to snore gently and then twitch its back leg as if it was dreaming about running.

Uncle Shawn decided to pass his time by looking at the path ahead of him. He was particularly good at looking. And what he saw when he looked was very worrying. In the soft earth there were the paw prints of a young badger. First the paw prints had been walking, and then they had been turning, and then walking, then turning again. "Dear me," said Uncle Shawn. "There's a little badger lost somewhere." And when Uncle Shawn stood up and walked and looked further up the path, he saw the small paw prints keep walking and wandering, and then… "Oh, dear. That's not good." There were the marks of great big horrible boots, slapping down angrily at the ends of some huge person's feet, and then the boot prints were stomped on top of the paw prints. And there was a smell of horribleness and stale pies. And there was a place where two little paws had scrabbled and tried to get away from something. "Well, that's not good." And then the paw prints disappeared. And the boot prints went back the way they'd come, only they seemed to be sinking into the earth a bit more than they had – as if the boot-wearer was heavier by about the weight of a kidnapped badger.

BADGER PAW PRINTS,
A GUIDE

WALKING

TURNING

MORE WALKING

MORE TURNING

GETTING PRETTY LOST

GETTING VERY LOST

HORRIBLE BOOTS STOMPING DOWN ON TOP OF INNOCENT PAW PRINTS THAT WERE SIMPLY MINDING THEIR OWN BUSINESS, HONESTLY...

Uncle Shawn shivered. Uncle Shawn frowned. Uncle Shawn shook his head and folded his arms. "That needs something doing about it..." He frowned harder. "If that doesn't need something doing about it, then I'm not Uncle Shawn."

He checked the name sewn inside his jacket, which said *UNCLE SHAWN*. "And I am Uncle Shawn!" He grinned. "So I must plan a plan – a rescuing plan." He felt in all his pockets, found a bit of toasted cheese finger and ate it thoughtfully. "Somewhere, there's a small badger in trouble…"

Uncle Shawn followed the footprints until they moved onto a big tarmac road and he couldn't follow any more. But this didn't mean he'd given up. He peered about so that he could remember the place before he went back to Paul the horse and got him to help search for the badger.

While he was peering about, Uncle Shawn noticed a hilltop in the west where it appeared to be raining incredibly hard, even though where he was standing the evening was warm and dry and pleasant. He noticed – because he was particularly good at noticing – that there were four llamas on the hill. "Hmmm…" hummed Uncle Shawn. "Llamas are unusual in these parts. And those llamas look unhappy." Even though the llamas were very far away, Uncle Shawn could recognize an unhappy llama when he saw one. "And they look as if they are homesick. And wet. And it seems they have nowhere nice and dry to keep cosy. That's not right." He patted and tugged at his wavy hair and pondered. "Something should be done about that... So... I'll need another plan..."

A GUIDE TO LLAMA MOODS

HAPPY LLAMA   SAD LLAMA

He also noticed that the sun was setting beautifully behind the pine trees and that three young squirrels – one of whom Uncle Shawn suspected still had his sock – were enjoying the view and singing about it. He shuffled his feet and said softly to no one, "How lonely it is to see such a good sunset and have no one to watch it with me. And how sad it is to have never met anyone who is good at jokes." He had another think to himself and then murmured, "That's a lot of things that need something doing about them … and maybe not much time to do them in … and there are a lot of plans to plan…" And then he grinned the biggest grin he had ever grinned. "And so I will start now." He began running on his long, long legs back towards Paul the horse. "I will do my best and then a bit better than that, and it will be a real adventure!" And he ran faster than he ever had done and felt excited and scared and brave and tall and happy, all at once. "I do hope we all get a happy ending and that nothing terrible happens…" And he ran even faster and made whooping noises. This surprised the siskins. 🐾

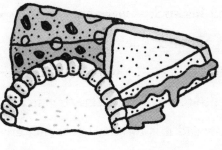

NASTY ➚
MCGLOONE
FOOD

SECTION FOUR

In which we meet all of the dreadful McGloones,

who are almost too horrible to mention.

We do have to mention them, though.

While the sun set gently and Uncle Shawn raced towards the start of his adventure, over in the west, the McGloone Farmhouse kitchen was filling with McGloones. Every one of the McGloones was there: Farmer McGloone and his wife, Myrtle McGloone, and the little McGloones, who were called Fred, Dusty, Bettina, Socket Wrench and Small. Farmer McGloone was also joined by his two sisters, Maude and Ethel, who we've met already.

That made nine McGloones.

FARMER McGLOONE
LIKES TO MAKE KITTENS INTO MITTENS

MYRTLE McGLOONE
A VERY AGGRESSIVE KNITTER

MAUDE AND ETHEL McGLOONE
VERY FOND OF PIES. NOT VERY FOND OF BADGERS.

FRED McGLOONE
DOESN'T SAY MUCH

DUSTY McGLOONE
WRITES TERRIBLE POEMS
ABOUT TRAINS

BETTINA McGLOONE
SHOUTS AT CLOUDS

SOCKET WRENCH
McGLOONE
SMALL BUT VIOLENT

SMALL
BITES OLD
LADIES ON
THE SHIN

Even one McGloone was really one too many
to have in a kitchen, or anywhere else. They were
clumsy, noisy, smelly, selfish and greedy. As well
as being cruel, they enjoyed watching other people being cruel when they were feeling too tired
to be cruel themselves. And they liked eating.

They were also very fond of being ignorant. If they didn't already know something, then they weren't interested in finding out about it – unless it might make someone cry.

The McGloone sisters were sneering as if they might be struck down dead by the furniture at any minute and as if they had never seen any-where so filthy and dreadful as the farmhouse kitchen. They did this because they hated Myrtle McGloone with all their hearts and they wanted her to feel like a bad housewife.

The sisters didn't usually set foot in the farm-house, but now they had been summoned for a family meeting and were all dressed up in their fin-est clothes. They wore matching purple gumboots with brown llama-fur trimming, pink tweed skirts, green blouses, orange knitted waistcoats and large, dusty hats decorated with flowers and a few veg-etables to replace the flowers that had fallen off over the years. They looked like a jumble sale and smelled of sprouts, but they were standing next to the greasy farmhouse stove and trying to look like duchesses. They were guessing this would mean making their mouths very narrow and tutting and waving their arms about so that their pink plastic handbags slid up and down their leathery big arms. This did make them look a little bit like some duchesses, but mostly they were just frightening.

Myrtle McGloone was sitting at the kitchen table and pretending the sisters weren't there.

MCGLOONE TABLE MANNERS – AN ILLUSTRATED GUIDE

This was difficult because Ethel's handbag kept hitting her on the back of her head. All the rest of the McGloones were squeezed nastily in round the table. They were jabbing each other in the ribs and shoving slices of lardy cake, jam sandwiches and apple pasties into their big McGloone mouths. And they were all shouting, so wet crumbs and bits of pasty were flying all over the place and sticking to things.

Farmer McGloone – who really didn't have any first name apart from Farmer – was shouting loudest of all. "The llamas aren't producing enough wool! And they're getting fat too slowly!"

Maude shouted back, "Well it was a ssstupid idea to bring them here! I told you ssso!"

"Don't you call my husband stupid!" yelled Myrtle, forgetting to ignore Maude. "You've got sprouts all over your hat! That makes you even stupider than a stupid old llama – you big snake!"

"Sssproutsss are the most fashionable vegetable

for hatsss!" Maude screamed happily – she loved a good argument. "You're jealousss of how lovely we are, that'sss your trouble!" And her wet and snaky hisses splashed everybody while she yelled.

"Now then, my pets," bellowed Farmer, while his children ate and punched each other. "You are all lovely, elegant and dainty." He stared at Myrtle, Ethel and Maude while he told them this and didn't appear to notice that they were as lovely, elegant and dainty as a donkey trying to ride a see-saw.

Under the cobwebby beams of the ceiling hung bottled spiders and rusty dog collars and lots of boiled bones tied up with ribbons and many, many grubby pie dishes – exactly as if the kitchen was some-times used to bake many, many pies. 🐾

SINISTER PIE CRUMBS ↗

REALLY NASTY LLAMA FOOD

SECTION FIVE

In which Brian Llama hears something very horrible and doesn't know what to do when he was already as miserable as a llama can be. This bit is quite scary.

Meanwhile, Brian Llama was walking along, dragging his tired hooves. In his mouth he was holding the handle of a solitary, tiny bucket of dinner that was supposed to be shared among four growing, hungry llamas. The bucket was half-filled with old cabbage leaves and crusts and Farmer McGloone's toe nail clippings and bacon rinds. This wasn't nice and wouldn't suit the llamas at all. Everyone – except the McGloones – knows that llamas are vegetarian. Farmer McGloone didn't believe in feeding the llamas anything expensive and said that leftovers would help their wool get longer. And he'd been getting more and more angry with the llamas for not growing their wool fast enough so that Myrtle could shear it off even faster and knit it into McGloone's Luxury Llama Wool Socks. He used the llamas' prize-winning poems to advertise the socks and put his own name at the bottom of each one, which wasn't fair, because he hadn't written them.

MCGLOONES

WET BITS
OF FOOD

BRIAN

Brian needed to cough so he put down the
bucket. This meant he was standing under the
farmhouse window at exactly the right moment
to hear something terrifying.

The window was open and there were wet bits
of food spattering out through it like nasty snow.
Brian couldn't help listening to the McGloones…

"I want jam, Ma! I want more jam!" bawled Dusty.

"Yes, I'm hungry! Is there any trifle?" yelled Bettina.

Each of the children was hungry and most of them were shouting for their favourite food in high, sneaky McGloone child voices. "I want dumplings! I want them right now! Or I'll bite you!" They didn't say please. McGloones don't.

Then Mrs McGloone yelled, "No more dumplings, you monsters! We've run out!"

"I hate you!" yelled back Socket Wrench.

"And I hate you all!" screamed their mother. "You're as bad as those ungrateful llamas. They aren't even trying to grow wool for us. I've only had enough to make twelve pairs of socks this week! And we do nothing but cherish them and pamper them!"

Farmer McGloone yelled then, "But never mind, dearest. On Saturday morning, we shall

take them out of the field and get rid of them, slish-slash. And then we can go to the badger fight. And then we'll make their meat into delicious llama stews and puddings and dumplings, and especially llama pies, and we'll make their skins into lovely wallets and shoes and a special handbag for you, dearest – and you children can have their eyes to nibble on with gravy. Won't that be grand?"

Brian Llama couldn't believe his wet, sheared ears. He didn't want to be a wallet, even a lovely one. And how would he see if his eyes had been nibbled? He didn't bother to pick up the bucket of rotten food – he wasn't feeling hungry any more. He just ran as quietly as he could with his shaking knees, all the way back to the other llamas. It was Thursday night. That only left Friday … and then… Slish-slash, stew and maybe handbags. Brian was now absolutely the most depressed and disappointed llama ever. He didn't know what to do. 🐾

TINY BLACK-AND-WHITE CAT

SECTION SIX

In which the little McGloones intend to spend a whole day being as horrible as usual, but then end up not being very nasty at all, because they get interrupted. And Uncle Shawn studies the McGloone Farm because he is making plans. And we hope he can hurry up, because he doesn't have much time to save everyone.

The following morning, an extremely tall, thin person with gingery-browny, wriggly hair and very blue eyes was walking along the lane to the McGloone Farm. It was Uncle Shawn. Last night, he had followed the faint smell of horribleness and boots – with a trace of pies – almost all the way to the McGloone Farm. Uncle Shawn guessed that might be the same farm where he'd seen those very sad llamas. But it had been too dark to do anything, so he had sneaked away again and stayed awake all night, pondering and puzzling and planning. As soon as the sun rose, he had rushed back to the farm in order to find out just a little bit more about the place and what might go on there.

While he marched along, he considered how llamas might have ended up on a wet hill. And he also considered the size of the boot prints and therefore the size of the big bullying person who had snatched up the little badger.

Some of his thoughts were making him furious, but he was managing to seem calm and was waving a stick of rhubarb to keep off the flies. He studied that far hillside where it was still raining, even though everywhere else was hot and dry. The llamas were up there, the four of them, huddled together. "What would it be like," Uncle Shawn asked himself, "to have a llama as a friend? Or four llamas?" He thought he could be very fond of llamas, even though he hadn't ever met one. "And what would it be like to be a cold, wet llama very far from home?"

Uncle Shawn reached the rusty, big sign by the farm entrance that read:

McGLOONE FARM
TO STAY HAPPY, WARM & SMART
SOCKS WOULD PLEASE
A LLAMA'S HEART

This was part of Guinevere's sock poem and she would have been very cross to know that it had been stolen.

Suddenly, out from the farmyard raced a tiny black-and-white cat. Then round the corner came the McGloone children, all rushing along towards Shawn and throwing stones at the cat, which hid behind Uncle Shawn's legs and peeped out at them.

The children saw Uncle Shawn and stopped. They were keen to keep on trying to hit the cat with stones, but Uncle Shawn's sparky eyes worried them a bit. And when he grinned, his grin somehow made them close to being scared.

"Good morning," said Uncle Shawn.

"Go away! You smell!" said the McGloone children. They also said, "Bandy legs!" and "We hate you!" and "Fish face!"

"What fine, loud voices you have," said Uncle Shawn. "I am Uncle Shawn."

"We don't care who you are!" said Bettina McGloone.

"I see you have stones in your hands," said Uncle Shawn politely. "Are they for throwing at cats?"

The McGloone children just stared at him, in case he was going to try to get them into trouble. Whenever somebody got them into trouble, the McGloone children would just laugh and then kick them and try to steal their wallets. But they had a feeling this might not be a wise thing to try with Uncle Shawn.

Uncle Shawn continued very gently, "Yes, I think they are for throwing at cats. You would want to be careful about that."

"Why?" said Socket Wrench, the biggest McGloone child, who was named after Farmer McGloone's favourite wrench. Socket Wrench picked up a fresh, very pointy stone and glowered. "You're going to get a stone bouncing off your head." And Socket Wrench McGloone smirked.

"Well ... I don't know about that," replied Uncle Shawn quietly. And then his whole face became very serious and anybody sensible would have thought twice about stones and throwing them ever again. But the McGloones were not sensible.

Uncle Shawn continued, "But I do know that sometimes the Great Grandfather Cat waits until midnight and comes and finds the people who throw stones at his grandchildren and then he sharpens his long, icy claws on their walls and they think, 'What's that scraping noise that sounds like kitchen knives outside and coming closer?' And then maybe he howls for a while and they think, 'What's that howling noise that sounds like a whole pack of wolves outside and coming closer?' And then the Great Grandfather Cat climbs up to their windows and they think, 'What's that thumping noise that sounds like enormous paws outside and coming closer?' And then the Great Grandfather Cat squeezes into their houses and opens his eyes very wide and stares at them..." Uncle Shawn opened his eyes very wide and stared at the McGloone children. And leaning around his left ankle, the little cat stared at them, too.

"Then what?" asked the littlest McGloone child, who was called Small, because by the time he arrived his parents had run out of names and couldn't think of anything else, apart from Small McGloone. He was quite scared about the Great Grandfather Cat by this time. "What happens?"

THE GREAT GRANDFATHER CAT

SHARPENING CLAWS

HOWLING OUTSIDE

SQUEEZING
THROUGH WINDOWS

STARING AT PEOPLE
IN A TERRIFYING WAY

"No one really knows what happens after that..." said Uncle Shawn, bending down close to whisper frighteningly into Small's ear. "The people who have been stared at are never able to say anything, ever again. And their hair turns white."

After that, the McGloone children either dropped their stones, or forgot they were holding them. And then Uncle Shawn picked up the little cat and carried him away, perched on his shoulder, looking back at the McGloones and feeling much happier and safer.

Uncle Shawn strolled all around the farm, keeping away from the grown-up McGloones, but studying everything closely. And he sniffed the air a lot – and thought he could smell boots and horribleness and pies and... Yes! Badger! The little badger was here!

This made his heart go galloping in his chest, but he strolled slowly and calmly like a man who is interested in ugly farms.

The McGloone children followed him at a careful distance and shivered in case he turned round and stared at them again.

Uncle Shawn waved at Maude and Ethel as they screamed at each other in the sprout patch. They didn't notice him. He waved as Farmer McGloone cut down a small tree that had done him no harm, and then hopped about and shouted when it fell over and landed in the wrong place and squashed a stack of new sock boxes. Farmer McGloone didn't notice Uncle Shawn, either. Then Uncle Shawn ambled back down the path and left the farm, still carrying the little cat.

And by this time he had seen – and sniffed – all that he needed to.

A SMALL TREE THAT HAS DONE HIM NO HARM

FARMER McGLOONE

Behind him, the McGloone children watched him go and wondered if he might come back and worry them again, or stop them doing anything else they enjoyed. They were unhappy, so they all kicked each other until they felt better.

"I wish it was spring," said Socket Wrench. "Then we could stamp on little frogs, or smash birds' nests."

SOCKET WRENCH
McGLOONE'S HOBBIES

GROWING SPOTS

SHOUTING AT CLOUDS

NOSTRIL EXPLORATION

SILENT FARTING

The other McGloones nodded, but even the idea of doing those unpleasant things didn't really cheer them up.

SECTION SEVEN

*In which Badger Bill wakes up one day nearer to
his big fight and gets even more scared, although
he is brave and handsome. We also learn that
dashing and intelligent badgers brush their tails to
make them glossy, especially if they have especially
fine tails. Never tell a badger that he only has a
stumpy little tail and needn't bother brushing it
– that will upset him, or her. But not as much as
making her, or him do press-ups before breakfast.*

While Uncle Shawn was taking the little cat all
the way home to its mother, Badger Bill was trying to run back to his home.

As soon as Ethel opened the door of the cold tripe-storing barn where he'd had to sleep, Bill rushed out for freedom. But Maude bounded after him and caught him by his tail, which really hurt. Then she slapped both his ears until he was dizzy and sore.

"Bessst to get usssed to it, dearie. Thessse love tapsss will toughen you up for tomorrow'sss fight. And if you still feel like running – then you can run for usss. All day." Which was a kind of joke, so she laughed like a blocked sink.

After that, Ethel slapped his ears, too – and giggled. "And wear your red shorts."

"But they rub my knees," said Bill very quietly, "and they have no room for my tail."

"Put them on, dearie," grinned Ethel, "or I shall get my tripe knife and snip off your precious tail."

Then – while Uncle Shawn was drinking milk and eating sardines with the mother cat – Maude began Bill's training by forcing him to do press-ups. Press-ups are hard for badgers because they have short arms.

Then Ethel ordered him to run up and down inside the barn where the two sisters stored and made imitation tripe. The tripe was used for packing round pianos and filling out the bits in newspapers that would otherwise be blank, or for making speeches by important people much longer and more boring.

Uncle Shawn had passed quite close to the barn while the sisters had been arguing so loudly amongst the sprout plants. And all around the barn there had been a clear scent of misery – the kind of scent you would get if a harmless and golden-hearted badger had been locked up all night with nothing to sleep on or to keep him warm but scraps of old, crumpled tripe.

There had been no bed for Bill, no pillow, no mattress and no quilt with pictures of famous badgers on it, like he had in his bedroom.

After a few hours of running, Bill was a little bit warm, because of all the chasing back and forth in his boxing boots that were too small and hurt his paws. He had said nothing after Ethel had threatened to cut off his tail, because he didn't know how he would manage without it. It was one of his best features and when he was at home he brushed it every morning. He didn't believe that he would ever get home again, and he felt very cold and tiny when he remembered his tail brush and slippers and how he would make toast for breakfast every morning and crunch it down while he looked out of the window and imagined good adventures that didn't sting his ears.

GOOD ADVENTURE

BAD ADVENTURE

HORATIO BADGER

CANOEING ROUND THE HIMALAYAS

HAVING YOUR EARS SLAPPED EVERY MORNING

"I wanted exciting things to happen," he thought. "This isn't exciting. This is rotten and nasty and scary and hard."

And leaning over the wall at one side of the yard came the revolting faces of the revolting McGloone children. Uncle Shawn had put them into a bad mood and they slapped their meaty chins down on the top of the wall and glowered at Bill as he passed back and forth in the barn windows. They were meaty and angry and greasy and full of nastiness. (Very like the homemade pies they loved so much.)

Then from the other side of the farm, their mother screamed, "Breakfast! You thieving little earwigs! Have you done your chores?"

"No, you big bag of beetles," the little McGloones muttered. But they wanted breakfast and so they backed away from the wall, still eyeing Bill.

Bill heard Socket Wrench say, "Fresh pies soon for breakfast." And then they made snickering, giggling noises and left him. 🐾

BIG BAG OF
BEETLES

MYRTLE
McGLOONE

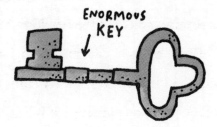

ENORMOUS KEY

SECTION EIGHT

In which we find out more than we want to about the McGloones' pie-making preparations. Readers who are sensitive should look away now until this bit has gone.

After breakfast, Farmer and Myrtle McGloone chased their children outside by trying to kick them and waving the rolling pin at their heads.

Then they opened up their biggest kitchen cupboard – the one with the well-oiled lock and enormous key. Then they peered inside and smiled at each other and rubbed their hands together happily, which made a noise like wet slippers.

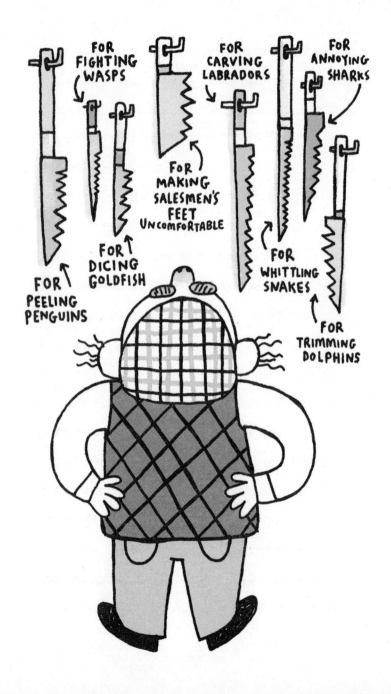

Inside the cupboard were rows and rows of knives: huge knives that were almost like swords, and middle-sized ones that were only as long as your arm, and small ones that you might use to peel a potato, and very tiny ones that seemed far too small to be useful for anything apart from maybe cutting the petals off daisies, or fighting wasps.

Farmer McGloone ran his huge, hairy fists along the handles of the knives. He knew exactly what each of them was for. The shine from the blades glimmered in his eyes and he chuckled and took his wife's hand. She kissed one of his leathery, wax-filled ears and sighed happily.

Farmer said, "I think llama pies will be good. Better than walrus, or giraffe, or panda..."

The McGloones had lured many animals to their farm from all over the world, simply to torment them and make them into pies.

Myrtle nodded. "And much less bother than gibbons."

"Yes, they were a terrible trouble. It was as if they didn't want to end up in chunks with gravy..." Farmer McGloone plucked a wiry hair from his earlobe and picked up a small knife that was made for peeling penguins. He pressed the very tip of the hair against the blade and it was immediately cut clean in half lengthways. "Yes. Nearly sharp enough," he said. Then he pulled out the grinding stone with which he kept the knives as sharp as sharp and then sharper than that and sat down delightedly to make them all even sharper.

Myrtle watched him adoringly.

They truly were very nasty people. 🐾

GRINDING
KNIVES

BILL'S
LUNCH →

SECTION NINE

In which Badger Bill gets another nasty fright
and makes a number of wishes. And where is
Uncle Shawn when Bill needs him? And Friday is
nearly all over and tomorrow it will be Saturday,
when bad things are going to happen...

Bill's lunch had not involved pies – which was just as well – but it hadn't been nice. It was only some raw, stale eggs in a mug with something green and lumpy mixed in. "Good for a fighter, dearie, drink it down," Ethel had said, and then she hadmade him lift weights and gave him a rope to skip with, when he was no good at skipping

because badgers' legs are very shapely and elegant in their way, but not long.

By the time Bill couldn't step or skip or lift any more, it was beginning to get dark. Ethel picked him up by his feet and carried him through to a small, secret-feeling yard, where Maude was waiting. She clapped her big, bacony hands together when she saw him and pointed to the large wire-mesh cage that took up most of the available space. "Here'sss where you'll be fighting, dearie!" Maude gurgled with laughter. "Won't he, Sssissster?"

Ethel unlocked a door in the cage and tossed Bill inside as if he was very unimportant and alone – which was how he felt.

"Enjoy yourssself, dearie. You'll be having fun sssoon..." said Maude.

Inside the cage was a small plate of stale tripe sandwiches and next to that was a tin mug of water. That was all the dinner Bill was going to get, but he didn't really mind, because he felt sick with worry and didn't want to eat anything. He wanted to curl up into a little ball the way he had in bed when he was a baby badger. He wished very hard that everything would go back to normal and be all nice again, and he closed his eyes and crossed his fingers...

And nothing happened.

And when he opened his eyes again he was still in a cage and still nearly at the end of Friday and still really, really sad all over. He sighed.

This made the sisters laugh – there were few things they found more amusing than someone being unhappy and sighing. And then the sisters left him, their identical orange and lime-green tweed skirts and massive purple cardigans giving him a headache on top of everything else.

BILL'S CAGE

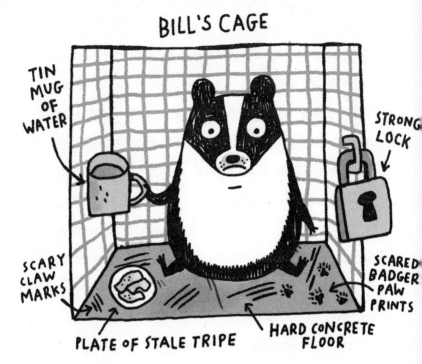

TIN MUG OF WATER

STRONG LOCK

SCARY CLAW MARKS

SCARED BADGER PAW PRINTS

PLATE OF STALE TRIPE

HARD CONCRETE FLOOR

Bill sighed again and turned round and round, trying to see if there was any way out of the cage. Badgers are excellent at digging, but the floor was made of hard concrete. And the concrete had marks on it that looked like the footprints of other sad badgers' feet. And there were the scrapes of the paws of something else, something with big claws...

Then he heard a noise.

He glanced up and there was a huge steel-grey

dog, with his gigantic, bristly muzzle right against the wire of the cage.

This wasn't a nice dog that you might play fetch with, or who would take you for a walk in the park, or show you how to cover every inch of yourself in mud just the way you should to prove that you've had lots of fun. This was the kind of dog who would only fetch you horrible things and try to bite you for fun and lie all the way along your furniture and not let you sit on even a tiny bit of it.

The dog growled and laughed. "Grrrrr ... harrharrharrharr. I've never seen anyone so pathetic." The dog licked his lips and his nose both at once, because they were very close together and some dogs do that kind of thing. "Hrrrhrrrgrrr. It won't take me more than a minute to finish you off." The dog shrugged his shoulders and wriggled his back so that Bill could see that he was made of muscles and then covered in more muscles with some extra muscles on top. The dog was all muscles – except for the parts of him that were teeth – and big claws. "Eatchya for breakfast. And they'll make a pretty little pie out of what's left. They do it most Saturdays."

"Um…" Bill was a polite badger and also didn't want to annoy the dog. "I'm Bill. Hello." Then he thought it might be better if he sounded fierce, so he tried to make his voice low and growly. "That is… That is…" Only this just made him cough and sound very squeaky afterwards. "Kkcagh… Kkcagh… I'm Battling Bob Badger. I think."

"You said you were called Bill." The dog sniggered. "Don't you even know your own name?"

"Bob is my fighting name." Bill tried to say this as if he was really tough, but it just made the dog laugh so hard that it had to roll on to its back and wave its legs in the air. "Ah…" Bill tried to be friends, in case that might help. "Who are you, Mr Dog?"

"Hrrrhrrr. Mr Dog… Fighting name…

Harrharrhurr..." The dog was crying, he was laughing so much.

In the end, the huge beast got its breath back, stood up and snarled, "I'm Ripper. And my brother is called Snapper. And my other brother is called Cracker."

Bill swallowed. "What imaginative parents you must have had."

"What does that mean?" Ripper stared at Bill as if he wanted to eat clever badgers more than anything else in the world. "Are you making fun of me?"

RIPPER

"Not at all. Not a bit. No, no, no... Ah, do your brothers live here, too, Mr Ripper?"

The dog licked his own nose again. "Oh, we all live here and we all fight here. We'll all be fighting you."

"What?" Bill could feel the white stripes on

BATTLING BOB BADGER
(8lbs, 6oz)
★ ★ ★ VS ★ ★ ★
YOUR FAVOURITES

SNAPPER — 40lbs, 5oz
CRACKER — 25lbs
RIPPER — 35lbs, 1oz

TICKET PRICE INCLUDES: Interval Entertainment & 1 FRESH-BAKED PIE

BET HOW LONG BOB CAN LAST!

his face fur getting much whiter and wider. "But that's not fair. I mean... There's only one of me..."

"I can count! I know there's only one of you!" Ripper snapped his jaws together with delight. "Who cares about fair? We brothers just want a bite of warm badger. Like last week.

Mmmmggrrrr. Nothing like a tasty bite of warm and tender badger."

"I'm not warm."

"You will be warm once we've chased you. Hrrr, hrrrr, harrharrharrharr."

"Well, I'm all stringy and full of gristle. My whole family are lumpy," lied Badger Bill.

"Oh, you'll be tender once we've thumped you. And we chew bricks to keep our teeth hard, so we like lumps. Harrharrharrharr." And Ripper leaned his muzzle against the wire mesh again and shouted, "Boo!"

This made Bill jump, even though he knew it made him look scared. Then Ripper trotted away, singing a little song: "Badger pies are made with eyes and knees and toes and whiskers – we love 'em so bisscause – we doooo…" Which didn't rhyme properly, but Bill thought he shouldn't say so in case it made Ripper even more cross and snarly and terrifying.

Badger Bill sat down, because he was feeling wobbly. He stared at his knees, which were shaking, and tried to think what he should do. He put one paw into the other, so that he could pretend he was holding someone else's hand, someone who could help him.

By now, the night had crept in, very apologetically, because it knew that it would worry Bill. After the night would come the morning … and it would be Saturday … and that would be the scariest day of all.

Bill looked up at the clear, twinkling sky and wished he had learned the names of the stars properly, and knew that he really, really, really needed a friend.

HORRIBLE WEATHER →

← LLAMA TEARS (ACTUALLY RAIN)

SECTION TEN

In which the llamas discover that they are
not very good at making escape plans and
cry a lot. Where is Uncle Shawn? It's even
nearer to Saturday than it was before...

On the other side of the farm, the llamas were
also looking up at the stars. It was easy for them
to see the whole sky because they had to sleep
outside, lying down in the damp grass. Their
view was a bit wet and misty, though, because of
the rain and because they were all crying. Brian
Llama had told them all about being made into
pies and wallets and things and each of them

felt cold and scared right into their backbones – which is a horrible way to feel.

"Oh, dear," sighed Guinevere Llama, "we must be able to think of ways to escape. We're intelligent llamas." She caught sight of Brian Llama and changed her mind. "Well, we're all llamas, anyway. Llamas are known for being wild and wily and for scaling walls and digging secret tunnels."

"No, we're not," said Brian Llama. "We're known for having wool and spitting at people."

"Except we've got almost no wool left and I've been crying too much to be able to spit at anyone," moaned Carlos Llama. "I don't want to be a wallet. Or a pie. I don't even *like* pie."

"What if we disguised ourselves as cows and slipped away?" suggested Ginalolobrigida Llama.

Brian sighed. "We don't have cow disguises. And four cows trying to catch a bus or get on a train would attract too much attention."

"We could phone for a cab," said Ginalolobrigida Llama.

"We're llamas – we don't have any money for a cab," snapped Brian.

"And we don't have phones, either," said Guinevere, which was very clever of her, but also very sad and unhelpful.

"Then why don't we climb over the electric fences?" asked Carlos Llama.

Brian sighed even harder. "Because they're electric. They're very dangerous – one jolt from them would turn you into burned toast – big, llama-shaped toast. Only one of us gets out at a time through the gate to fetch the food. And the electricity is always kept turned on – you can hear it sizzling."

Carlos sniffled. "I'm sorry, I'm so tired and cold that I forgot."

The other three llamas drooped their heads and started crying again. Brian tried to cheer them up.

BURNED LLAMA TOAST

"Look, maybe I could escape the next time I go to get the food and then maybe I could find someone who would help us and maybe..." But he couldn't really think where he would go and he didn't know anybody in the whole of Scotland except the McGloones. He also knew that llamas are very tall and obvious – even at night – and someone would recognize him and send him back.

ELECTRICITY-
PROOF RUBBER
SUIT

HOT PORRIDGE
WITH BANANAS
& RASPBERRIES

At that point, Farmer McGloone came to the big fence at the foot of the field, wearing his bright red electricity-proof rubber suit and gloves and carrying his small, mean torch to show him the way over the bumpy, wet grass. He opened up the gate with his gloves and walked in, shouting at the llamas, "Come here, you big, daft lumps of llama – see what I've got for you." And he set down four enormous buckets of hot porridge with fresh raspberries and bananas in, which llamas love.

Brian was just about to shout, "Quick, we can

overpower him and then perhaps steal his car! Except we can't drive! But we could try to! Or we could all push it!" But the other llamas were too excited by the first proper food they'd seen since they left Peru, and they rushed forward and started eating. And while they were in Brian's way, Farmer McGloone just slipped out through the gate and locked it again, and then grinned the grin of someone who has decided to fatten up his llamas so that they'll make better pies and bigger wallets.

It was far too late for this to work, but Farmer McGloone was very stupid and also very mean. He would never have fed the llamas properly for even a week – it would have cost too much.

Brian looked at Farmer McGloone's big, yellowy teeth shining in the light of the stars and the torch. Brian shuddered and tried not to think of what it would be like to be covered in pastry. And he tried not to think of a horrible McGloone voice saying "Slish-slash."

AWAKE →

SECTION ELEVEN

In which all our chums spend a sleepless night
for different reasons. And Uncle Shawn thinks
up almost the whole of a very good plan.

For the whole of Friday night – which he spent in
the draughty fighting cage – Badger Bill couldn't
sleep. He was scared and feeling sick. He was also
wondering if he could thump even one of the big
bullying dogs even a tiny bit before they ate him
all up. And he said to himself, "Oh, please, I need
a friend. I do. Maybe one with a helicopter. Or
some soup. Or a bed. Or just a sleeping bag. Or
a big woolly jumper."

A FRIEND
WITH A BED

A FRIEND WITH SOUP

A FRIEND WITH A BIG
WOOLLY JUMPER

A FRIEND WITH A
SLEEPING BAG

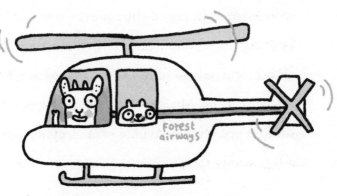

A FRIEND WITH A HELICOPTER

· · ·

And for the whole of Friday night – which they spent in the draughty wet field being rained on – the llamas couldn't sleep. They were scared and feeling sick.

Brian Llama whispered, "I wonder if the people who wear me as shoes will get sore feet because of the shoes being made of very unhappy llama leather..." And then he felt even sicker.

They were all very unhappy llamas. And Guinevere Llama said, "I hope everyone who uses us as wallets gets sore fingers."

And Carlos Llama said, "I hope everyone's belts are too tight and give them indigestion."

But that didn't cheer them up.

And for the whole of Friday night Uncle Shawn didn't sleep. He was busy. He drew all kinds of plans in chalk on the walls of the caravan where he was staying. The walls of the caravan were very dirty, so the chalk was very easy to see. And he whistled to himself and hummed and sometimes sang, because that helped him think. "Oh, the llamas and the badger must be freeee … and happeeee…" He wasn't very good at songs.

He also wasn't very good at making plans – they made his head spin. But he kept on pondering and mulling and puzzling anyway.

UNCLE SHAWN'S PLANS
↓

MOTHER MOLE

DISH OF SLUGS

And sometimes he would chat with the mother mole he had taken out of his pocket and who was eating a dish of slugs and listening to him. While she listened, she mainly shook her head at him and told him to start all over again. Which he did.

On the outside, Uncle Shawn's caravan was painted many kinds of colours, as if he couldn't decide which was his favourite and so wanted to have them all. It was a very nice wooden caravan and was drawn by Paul the horse – who didn't mind pulling it, because it was quite light and he was really strong.

And before the sun came up, Uncle Shawn went outside and woke Paul and whispered to him, "Here we go, then."

And Paul grumbled, "Already? Last time you woke me up you didn't even have a plan..."

"Well..." mumbled Uncle Shawn.

"Do you have a plan?" Paul didn't want to pull the caravan all the way over to the McGloones' for no reason and was always a bit grumpy when he'd just woken up.

"I have a sort of plan..." explained Uncle Shawn, pulling his fingers through his hair and making it wake up and wriggle as if it was having several ideas of its own. "Almost the whole of a plan. Or more than half. A good plan. An excellent probably plan ... it's nearly perfect ... I mean, I wouldn't want to give the game away." And he gave a little shuffle with his feet and winked.

Paul couldn't see the wink, because it was still dark, and he thought this was all too disorganized.

"This is all too disorganized," he said, and he huffed with his whiskery, horsey lips, the way that horses do when they think you might not have a clue what you're doing.

Uncle Shawn patted Paul to make him feel better. "Yes, but if we don't set off now, we won't be in time and if we're not in time we'll be too late ... and if we get there soon enough and we are in time and my plan works and then the bits I haven't quite tidied up yet also work and nothing goes wrong and we don't make any mistakes and the wind is from the south-west and we cross our fingers ... then we could do amazing things."

"I don't have any fingers. I'm a horse," said Paul. He wasn't always the jolliest horse to take on a life-saving adventure.

"Well, that's true," said Uncle Shawn. "Could you cross your eyes instead?"

"Only if you want me to pull the caravan in the wrong direction." Paul huffed again. "I shall just wish us luck. Because I feel we shall need it. A lot."

Uncle Shawn jigged about a little because he was excited and in a hurry. "Well, luck would be very handy. Thank you. And maybe we won't be taken prisoner, or locked up and then covered in gravy and nibbled, or put into pies. And even if we are – it will have been an adventure. I've always wanted an adventure. An adventure with friends."

MOTHER MOLE PIE   PAUL THE HORSE PIE

UNCLE SHAWN PIE ?!

And so Paul shook his head and huffed some more, but then started to pull the caravan very quietly. He had already told Uncle Shawn to wrap his hooves in pieces of blanket and old pullovers, and so he didn't clip and he didn't clop. And the wheels of the caravan had been oiled so that they didn't squeak and didn't squook. And Uncle Shawn walked along beside Paul with his mahogany shoes around his neck so that he would be extra stealthy, because that was part of the plan. And he thought to himself that it was excellent to be going on an adventure and to have (most of) a plan for amazing things. 🐾

PAUL ↓ MANY COLOURS ↓ ↙ WOODEN CARAVAN

↑ HOOVES WRAPPED IN BLANKET AND OLD PULLOVERS

PULLING OUT HIS WHISKERS →

SECTION TWELVE

In which Uncle Shawn and Badger Bill
meet for the very first time, but Bill
doesn't quite get rescued. Not yet... But
that's all part of the plan. Maybe.

By the time it was just before dawn on Saturday, Badger Bill hadn't slept one bit, not for the whole night. And he had spent so long pulling at his whiskers with worry that they'd almost come loose. From somewhere not very far away, he could hear McGloone shouting and McGloone laughing and the clumping of McGloone boots and a noise that sounded like what you might hear if someone was sharpening big knives. This all made his tummy feel bad.

He could also smell a strange scent – as if there was a horse and a tall person nearby. And he could hear the sound of something very big making no sound at all. This was confusing and on top of all his other fears and confusions it made his head hurt. "This will be horrible," he said to himself. "I don't want to get thumped and then eaten and I especially don't want to get thumped and then eaten when I have a headache." He snuffled and wiped his nose on the back of his paw because he didn't have a handkerchief. (He was a neat badger.) "I do wish I had even just one friend. Just one."

Then, while he was staring sadly at the bales of tripe next to his cage, he saw the light from a torch. And something gingery and wriggly was sneaking and darting behind the tripe bales. He wondered whether this was some new, very

WHAT'S BEHIND THE TRIPE BALES?

COULD IT BE...

① A FEROCIOUS GINGER DOG?

② AN ENORMOUS GINGER CAT?

③ AN ENORMOUS GINGER CAKE?

ferocious tall ginger dog that was going to tease him. "Oh dear..." thought Bill. Then he noticed a pair of very blue eyes looking at him from out of the shadows.

And now he could smell toffee and helpfulness and the torchlight was shining into his cage.

"Ow." And straight into his eyes, which made them hurt.

And then a voice that sounded like a good voice whispered, "Sorry." And the torch shone back on a stranger's face and those two blue eyes. One of the eyes winked happily.

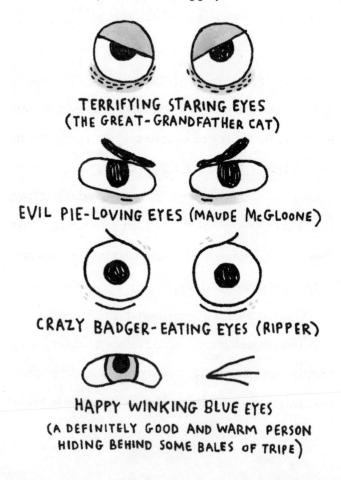

TERRIFYING STARING EYES
(THE GREAT-GRANDFATHER CAT)

EVIL PIE-LOVING EYES (MAUDE McGLOONE)

CRAZY BADGER-EATING EYES (RIPPER)

HAPPY WINKING BLUE EYES
(A DEFINITELY GOOD AND WARM PERSON
HIDING BEHIND SOME BALES OF TRIPE)

Bill whispered to himself, "Something that wanted to thump me and eat me wouldn't wink at me ... at least, I don't think so." And Bill kept looking at the eyes and they looked back at him and he thought that these were the friendliest eyes he had ever seen.

Bill started to feel a bit ... almost ... nearly ... happy.

Then Bill heard a definitely good and warm and kind sort of voice whisper, "You are not going to be thumped or eaten. You are going to be rescued." And before Bill could ask any questions or say anything else at all, the whole of the tall, thin shape of Uncle Shawn jumped out fast from behind the tripe. Then he started to dance a highly peculiar dance.

"Oh, thank you," whispered Bill.

"You're welcome." Uncle Shawn jiggled and wiggled and stamped – Bill could hear feet banging and stamping. He could also see some of what

Uncle Shawn was doing because the torch was moving about and lit up jiggling elbows and bouncing knees and swinging ankles as they moved.

"Umm..." said Badger Bill. "Am I going to be rescued soon – because you seem to be just dancing..."

"Dancing and rescuing are the same thing. And I'm Uncle Shawn, by the way," announced Uncle Shawn, and then he stood on one leg and waved his free foot and then he did the same again, only the other way around. "Pleased to meet you." And he swayed his arms backwards and forwards like washing on a line.

"Er..." Badger Bill had been hoping for a team of men in balaclavas with grappling hooks or canoes to come and save him. This was all a bit odd. And he was still locked in a cage. "Well, I'm Badger Bill," he said. "William J. Badger for special occasions." Bill hoped this was a special occasion. He hoped it was when he would get out of the cage and end up safe and cosy and snuggled with hot chocolate and slippers and sandwiches with earthworms and peanut butter. Badgers love earthworms and peanut butter.

BADGER BILL's FAVOURITE FOODS

COCOA

BERRIES

HONEY ↑

TOASTED SLUGS ↗

PORRIDGE ↗

↑ TOASTED TOAST

CHEESE (<u>NOT</u> PIES !!!)

Uncle Shawn stopped dancing and grinned a huge grin as the sun started to rise. "Really? I have never had a friend called Badger Bill before. This will be wonderful." And then he skipped and hopped and then started to wriggle all over very fast, which made his hair wriggle even faster, so that it just looked like the colour red in a big blur all round his head. And the birds started to sing in a more than usually cheerful way, as if they knew something wonderful was happening.

But Bill – who was tired and still in his cage – had started to worry that this strange Uncle Shawn person was another McGloone who had just come to make fun of him. Although Uncle Shawn seemed much too nice to be a McGloone.

And then Uncle Shawn – who was a bit out of breath by now – announced, "I am dancing my Summoning Dance and this is the start of the rescue. I have a plan and everything. Mostly." He reached into his pocket and brought out a very dirty piece of paper with jam on it and lots of scribbles and some big letters which read: *PLAN*.

This did not make Bill feel happier. "But I need to get out right now. Before I have to fight one, or two, or probably three of the hugest dogs in the world." The idea of this made him miserable and shivery all over and his fur ruffled up sadly. "This is the start of Saturday."

"Oh, I'll be back before you need me. Honestly."

"Back? That means you're going! You can't go!" squeaked Badger Bill.

"I have to. But I will be back. Really. Trust me." Uncle Shawn's very blue eyes were really easy to trust. "And I'm so glad to meet you, William J. Badger, and I think we will be best friends. I really do. And remember – you never know what might happen until it's happened – so *don't worry*." And Uncle Shawn kept on dancing, but danced further and further away until he was out of the yard and had disappeared.

And Badger Bill slumped down where he was sitting and thought, "It's not much use starting to be someone's friend if you've only got part of a Saturday left before you're made into pies. He'll look silly holding a pie and telling people it's his best friend. And I'll be a pie... That won't be silly. That will be TERRIBLE."

Not far away, there was the sound of three enormous dogs starting to bark and shouting, "We're coming to get you! Hrrrr! Not long now! Hrraaarrr!" And then they laughed three enormous laughs. 🐾

SOUND FX:
WOODEN
STAMPING
NOISES

SECTION THIRTEEN

In which Uncle Shawn dances as no uncle has ever danced before. And it will turn out that this section is very unlucky for the McGloones because it contains their last chance and they miss it. They don't even notice when it goes by.

And Uncle Shawn danced furiously and happily and crazily and quickly and wildly. He danced beside the McGloones' farm, along this wall and that wall and then the other wall and the other wall over there. Uncle Shawn danced and danced until he was getting really hot and dizzy.

Since he'd put his shoes on to help with the

stamping parts of his dance, the McGloones could hear him, and eventually seven sausage-lipped, meat-eared McGloone faces were peering out of the window and looking at him.

Because they thought Uncle Shawn might be dancing because he was happy, and because they hated other people being happy (and because they were naturally rude), the McGloones shouted at him.

The McGloone children shouted, "You smell! We hate you!" And then Socket Wrench yelled, "Cat lover!" and Small bellowed, "Weird knees!" and Bettina screamed, "Big poo face!" Fred didn't shout anything. Fred never did.

And Mrs McGloone shouted, "You're trespassing! And there's an extra charge for dancing! You can't dance here unless you want to buy pies! Give us your money!"

And Uncle Shawn looked up as the sun rose higher in the sky and made his eyes seem very

THE (VERY SMELLY) MCGLOONE FARMHOUSE

fierce and shiny and he called back and asked, "Would those be llama pies and badger pies?"

And Farmer McGloone yelled, "Get on out of it, before I cut your ears off with my llama knives – coming round here and dancing and laughing without permission!"

And for a moment Uncle Shawn looked up at all of their oily, hating eyes and he said quietly, "Well, you did have a chance to do better and be nicer and kinder. Everyone does..." And then he nodded and danced away from the farmhouse and along the path that led to the llama's field, stamping so hard that a big cloud of dust followed him. 🐾

BIG DUST CLOUD

GRAVY AND MOUSE EARS

SECTION FOURTEEN

In which Badger Bill gets almost more worried
than a badger can and the McGloone sisters wear
clothes that should be illegal in all sensible countries.
And you never know what might happen until it's
happened. And this is when it will start to happen.

The two dreadful sisters had eaten a hearty breakfast of gravy and mouse ears in their own damp
and ugly house behind the tripe barn. Now they
were busy at the fighting cage. They were dressed
in their Saturday finest. Ethel was wearing a lem-
on-coloured silk miniskirt – which showed off
her scaly and bumpy knees – and a puce velvet

top and red snakeskin high-heeled shoes. Anyone who'd seen her without expecting to would have screamed and been sick. And Bill felt like screaming and being sick anyway.

Maude was even more frightening. She was dressed in a wide, round skirt of purple chiffon and lace and bows and an orange leather jerkin and high-heeled pink-and-black cowboy boots. This made her look like something you might dream if you were feeling really ill.

Bill was feeling really ill, but he knew he wasn't dreaming. He was still locked inside the cage. Meanwhile, crowds of people were gathering. They were all parking their cars and walking to watch the badger fight, as they did every Saturday, unless it was too snowy or too wet.

Ethel and Maude were laughing and teetering about on their heels and shaking hands with lots and lots of people who were crowding into the little yard and sneaking looks into the cage and pointing at Bill and screeching with laughter.

It seemed that Bill's fight was going to be a popular event. He'd never been a popular event. He'd only had an audience once, when he'd recited a poem at school and forgotten the end. "I especially don't want an audience now," thought Badger Bill. "I want to be rescued! Where is that Uncle Shawn?"

But there was no sign of Uncle Shawn, only more and more people who were squeezing into the yard. In fact, there were visitors' cars parked right the way up the lane.

(Bill didn't know this, but just at that moment, Uncle Shawn was dancing along that very lane and slightly scratching the paintwork of each car as he went.)

"Place yer bets!" yelled Ethel. "Who thinks the badger will last three minutes?"

Maude yelled, too: "How long will the badger lassst? Do I hear forty ssssecondsss?"

Bill tugged at his shorts and scuffed his boots on the floor of the cage, and all of his insides seemed to be flapping about and interfering with his heart.

BILL'S INSIDES FLAPPING ABOUT

INTERFERING WITH HIS HEART

Suddenly, Ethel reached into her top and pulled out a surprisingly large bell, which she rang loudly and wildly. Then Maude screamed out, "THREE MINUTESSS TO GO, LADIESSS AND GENTLEMEN, BEFORE BATTLING BADGER BOB FACESSS RIPPER!" Many of the people in the crowd put up umbrellas while Maude hissed, because this produced a good deal of spray. "THE FAMOUSSLY SSSAVAGE RIPPER!"

At this point the crowd cheered.

"AND SSSNAPPER!" By now Maude's chin was dripping with saliva – as if she was a snake trying to drink lemonade and missing.

The crowd cheered some more.

SALIVA

120

"AND CRACKER!"

There was a huge, final cheer and then Bill could see that everyone in the yard was shuffling or jumping out of the way to leave a wide path that led between the entrance of the yard and the fighting cage.

Then, with a flash of claws and far too much barking, Ripper pranced in, snapping and glaring. He was bigger than Bill remembered. His coat was gleaming and his claws and teeth were shining and clattering.

Ripper was followed by Snapper – who was even bigger than Ripper – and who growled like a cellar full of lawnmowers and tried to bite someone's trousers.

And then – Badger Bill couldn't believe it – here came Cracker. He was only a little bit taller than Bill. He had quite small paws and quite short claws. But when Bill looked into his eyes he knew that Cracker was the scariest animal you could meet and that he had no mercy and would punch grandmothers and nip off squirrels' tails and steal ice cream from lonely orphans, just for fun.

The crowd fell silent.

Cracker always made crowds fall silent. Everyone he looked at flinched and backed away. Even his brothers seemed scared of him and his small, very, very sharp needle teeth and his tiny, very, very sharp claws and his big, nasty, nasty mind full of terrible ideas, all flickering about at the backs of his eyes. Meeting his eyes was like looking into two pools of hate that went down and down into forever.

Bill knew that in less than three minutes Cracker's eyes might be the last things he would see...

Maude came and unlocked the cage door and the dogs slowly approached it. Even Maude didn't like to be too close to Cracker and made sure that she didn't turn her back on him.

RIPPER!

SNAPPER!

2 POOLS OF HATE →

VERY VERY → SHARP NEEDLE TEETH

TINY, VERY VERY SHARP CLAWS ↙

CRACKER!

The human beings either side of the wire mesh stared down at Bill and nudged each other, saying things like, "That badger won't last long." And, "Small, isn't he?" And, "I think he's going to cry."

Bill was trying to stand up with his eyes shut because that might make it easier. But it didn't. He couldn't get up. He couldn't move any more, he was so frightened, and he thought that any moment now he wouldn't be able to breathe...

Only then something very strange took place,

which shouldn't have surprised Bill, because – as Uncle Shawn had said – you never know what might happen until it's happened.

First, there was a remarkable noise, as if thunder was thundering quite close and getting closer. Under poor Bill's feet, the concrete was shaking and starting to crack and there were louder and louder rumbles and bangs and clatters on all sides.

From the back of the crowd, a very tall, thin person, who Badger Bill now recognized, winked straight at him and then smiled. And then Uncle Shawn (because that's who it was, of course) shouted, "Look! Look! The farmhouse is falling down! Everything is falling down!"

Uncle Shawn had an incredibly loud voice when he wanted to and everyone could hear him, but for a little while no one believed him.

Ethel laughed. "That house has been there for years, what are you talking about—" But then she noticed that everyone else was turning towards the McGloone house, where Uncle Shawn was pointing, and she saw – as everyone else did – that the farmhouse's slimy, miserable bricks and nasty, bad-tempered stones were crumbling apart. The roof was sagging. One of the windows fell out, followed by two of the McGloone children. Slates began to fly through the air and shatter on the ground.

"That'sss not sssupposssed to happen!" screamed Maude, making a couple who had travelled all the way from Poole to see the badger fight very wet indeed.

As the bricks and beams and slates tumbled, the crowd started to rush about in panic, but it

BRICKS CRUMBLING

ROOF SAGGING

WINDOWS BREAKING

THE MCGLOONE FARMHOUSE IN (VERY SMELLY) BITS

was hard for them to know where they should run to. The farmhouse was falling apart and so was the barn and so was Ethel and Maude's house and so was every single wall that belonged to the McGloones. It was all crashing and clattering down, so that people were stubbing their toes on bricks and being covered in dust and thumped by bits of masonry and each other.

"Oh, wonderful! Wonderful!" Bill was sure that the fight wouldn't happen now and that he would be all right. And maybe this had something to do with Uncle Shawn, who was walking towards the cage as if he knew exactly what was going on and felt very safe about it. None of the bits and pieces of farmhouse and wall were falling anywhere near him. It was as if he was carrying a big invisible umbrella over his incredibly happy head.

But then Ripper and Snapper and Cracker – who were cowards when anything happened that they didn't understand – rushed into the cage because they thought it would keep them safe from falling lumps of McGloone Farm. Suddenly, Bill was faced by just the horrible faces his nice, quiet, peaceful face had never wanted to face.

As Ethel teetered past on her snakeskin stilettoes and Maude tottered past on her cowboy boots, Bill found himself squashed into a corner of the cage with three snarly mouths very close to him and drool dripping off snarly teeth and onto his fur. It was the worst thing yet. And Cracker was peering at him with his deep, deep black eyes full of wicked thoughts.

Only, just then a different kind of thunder that

STOLEN WIG

wasn't to do with walls collapsing got louder and louder and louder, and then the yard was packed with a rushing crowd of squirrels and rabbits and weasels and shrews and siskins and blackbirds and robins and every kind of small animal that was fond of Uncle Shawn. (And pretty much all the small animals that had ever met Uncle Shawn liked him very much.) The creatures hopped and scampered and leaped and scrabbled and flew and pecked their way among anyone who was still left in the yard. The couple from Poole had their ankles nibbled by shrews, and a man from Cumbernauld had his wig stolen by a young squirrel, who also laughed at him, and rolled-up hedgehogs rattled

about across the cobbles, prickling people for being so nasty and wanting to see a badger in shorts when everyone knows badgers don't like them.

And – thank goodness – while some of the creatures were clearing the yard, a big crowd of stoats and weasels and hedgehogs and the little cat and her mother all rushed right into the cage and swept Badger Bill out past the dogs.

The dogs were very surprised and scared and covered in sparrows, who were pecking their ears and then jumping out of the way of the dogs' teeth. And wasps were stinging them and giggling and stinging them again. As it happened, the dogs were horribly afraid of wasps and had always been nasty to them and squashed their nests while they were sleeping in the winter. So now the wasps were having their revenge. And Ripper and Snapper and Cracker were howling like puppies and big lumps were coming up on their noses and all over them under their fur.

THINGS THAT MAKE A WASP GIGGLE

BEING TICKLED

STINGING UNPLEASANT DOGS

EATING TOO MUCH ICE CREAM

WHERE DO YOU TAKE A SICK WASP? TO WASPITAL!

TELLING WASP JOKES

And in all this confusion, Badger Bill felt a big, warm, safe hand take hold of his paw and he looked up and saw Uncle Shawn smiling down at him and saying, "Everything is fine. But we have to run now."

And Bill did run, as fast as his lovely but slightly short legs would go. And the small animals and the little birds all ran and rushed and fluttered and buzzed away, too. And for a few moments Uncle Shawn turned round and ran backwards so that he could shout, "Thank you, wasps. Thank you, Jeremy Wasp. Thank you, Suzie Weasel. Thank you, Angus Rabbit and Mary Rabbit and Hughie Rabbit and Shane Rabbit... Thank you, Mother Mole. Thank you very much! Thank you all!" And the so many, many creatures scattered away into the countryside again, laughing and cheering and saying, "It was our pleasure! Don't mention it, Uncle Shawn!" Because they had never liked the McGloones, not one bit.

Behind Bill and Shawn, the last pieces of the farm and its buildings fell into a number of ugly heaps of rubble. 🐾

SECTION FIFTEEN

In which three dogs have a change of heart.
Don't worry, this is a very short section
and the excitement is still going on all over
McGloone Farm. We'll be back there soon.

And Ripper and Snapper and Cracker ran harder and faster than they had run in their lives until they were so far away they ended up at the seaside. Being at the seaside always cheers everyone up and makes them nicer to be around. After they reached the beach, the dogs didn't stop for ice cream – they swam out to sea. This was because their ears hurt and they thought the water would

THE DOGS' NEW SMALL ISLAND HOME

MINI GOLF

HAPPY DOGS

ICE CREAM SHACK

TIDE POOLS

SANDY BEACH

DRIFTWOOD TOYS

CHARMING PICNIC SPOT

help ease the pain. They kept on swimming until they came to a small island where there was nobody else.

And they lived there for the rest of their lives. For a while, they were still fairly horrible dogs and shouted at each other and ran about a lot while snapping and growling. But slowly they calmed down and explored the island and built nice kennels for themselves from washed-up

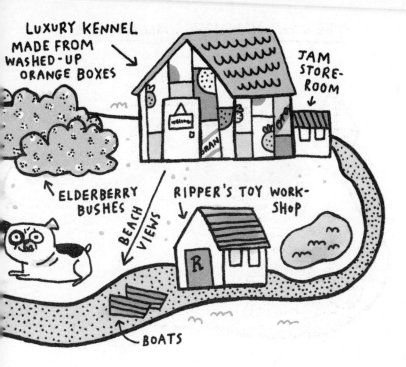

LUXURY KENNEL MADE FROM WASHED-UP ORANGE BOXES

JAM STORE-ROOM

ELDERBERRY BUSHES

BEACH VIEWS

RIPPER'S TOY WORK-SHOP

BOATS

orange boxes, and made toys out of bits of drift-wood. And without the McGloones to torment them, they turned into extremely peaceful and polite dogs. And when anyone came to call at the island, the dogs would help them get out of their boats and show them where the best places were to have picnics.

And if the dogs saw a wasp, they would feed it jam that they made out of elderberries. 🐾

SOUND FX:
LOUD SINKING
NOISES

SECTION SIXTEEN

In which there are some pants and some lemonade and Uncle Shawn forgets something very important. But Bill is really happy.

The McGloone Farm was, by now, mainly a number of heaps of rubble, and Bill was free. He was completely free. His heart was free in his chest and skipping in a way that made him feel sparkly. He was running next to Uncle Shawn.

"Wasn't that good?" Uncle Shawn chuckled as he loped across the grass, his long legs making it hard for Bill to keep up.

"That was... Yes, that was... But how did...?"

And Bill would have asked, "But how did you manage all of that?" Only then there was a lot of noise from where the cars were parked in the lane as each car slowly sank into gaps that opened up in the ground and swallowed them whole like shiny metal sweets.

"Good heavens!" said Bill.

"It was Mother Mole," explained Uncle Shawn. "I made a plan and she agreed with it, which was very nice of her. And I summoned her and all her mole relatives with my Summoning Dance and then they knew just where to dig, because I stamped to show them, and they made all the foundations of McGloone

MOTHER MOLE AND HER MOLE RELATIVES

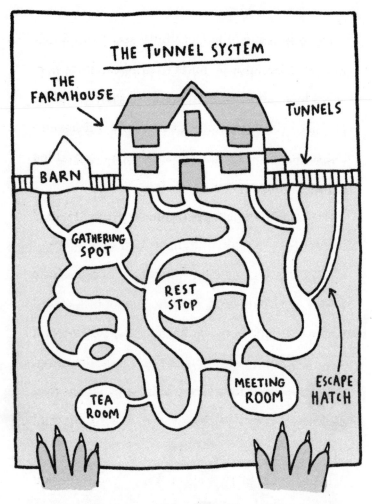

Farm turn into crumbles and dust. Clever moles. And clever me, actually." Uncle Shawn felt very proud of himself for making such a fine adventure happen.

By this time, Badger Bill was completely exhausted because he hadn't really eaten or slept for so long and his head went all twirly and he was glad to be rescued, but he really did have to stop running. So he did. He sat down fast and felt funny, but happy, but also a bit sick.

So Uncle Shawn stopped running, too. "Hello." He grinned. "Hello, William J. Badger."

Bill took lots of deep breaths and felt Uncle Shawn sit down next to him. Then Bill stared at his own feet because he felt shy, but he said softly, "Hello." And then he felt his face smiling, which it hadn't done since he'd been put in that horrible sack and so many horrible things had happened.

Then Uncle Shawn asked Bill, "What do you call a three-legged donkey?"

And Bill giggled and said, "A wonky." And then he asked Uncle Shawn, "What's orange and sounds like a parrot?"

And Uncle Shawn laughed and laughed and answered, "A carrot."

And Bill took off his painful, sad boxing boots and threw them away and wriggled his toes in the soft grass. He took off his tail-squeezing shorts that weren't half as lovely as his thick, glossy badger coat that he wore all the time and was all he needed. His fur was feeling much happier in every hair now that he was free. He sniffed all the interesting and tasty smells that were in the countryside around him. By now, he was smiling from his ears to his paws and Uncle Shawn gave him some lemonade out of a little bottle he'd brought with him as part of the plan in case anybody got thirsty. Bill drank it and it was the best lemonade in the world.

Bill was about to say, "Thank you for rescuing me. And for the lemonade," because he was a polite badger, but then Uncle Shawn shouted, "Oh, I knew I'd forgotten something!" And Uncle

BEST
LEMONADE
IN THE
WORLD

Shawn picked up Badger Bill and put him on his shoulders and put the lemonade bottle back into one of his baggy jacket pockets and then he stood up and started sprinting very hard.

"What? What have you forgotten?" asked Badger Bill, who could hear something worrying behind him and smell something familiar and very, very unpleasant getting closer... "What!?!?"

"Oh, I just forgot that we would have to keep running because the McGloones would work out all this was my fault and want to make me into pies as well as you, and then there are the llamas to consider…"

"What?!?!"

And, sure enough, when Badger Bill turned a little to check, every one of the McGloones – Farmer McGloone, Mrs McGloone, Socket Wrench McGloone, Dusty McGloone, Small McGloone, Fred McGloone, Bettina McGloone, Ethel McGloone and Maude McGloone – were chasing along and waving jagged parts of window frames and knives and fists and stones. Ethel and Maude had taken off their shoes, and their yellowy, leathery feet were slapping on the ground with each step. Several young squirrels were skipping around the sisters' ankles and laughing at them, because their skirts had been torn and their big, grey pants were showing.

SAD
LLAMA

SECTION SEVENTEEN

In which Badger Bill is mistaken for someone taller
and there is a great deal of running. And some
shouting. The McGloones don't get what they
expected and Uncle Shawn runs out of plan and
then finds some more plan and many things happen
all at once. And there is a great deal of mud.

Meanwhile over in the llama field it had actually stopped raining, even though the llamas had definitely seemed to hear thunder coming near, which they thought was odd.

"Well, this is a nicer day," said Carlos Llama.

"I don't want to be killed and made into pies

143

DOWNHEARTED LLAMAS →

ELECTRIC FENCE ↓

on a nice day," said Guinevere Llama. "Then I'll miss it."

"I don't want to be killed at all," said Brian Llama.

"Especially not with my fur in this condition," said Ginalolobrigida Llama.

The llamas had been too downhearted to notice Uncle Shawn dancing very carefully round the whole of their field as the sun rose. They also hadn't noticed the cloud of dust hanging above what had been McGloone Farm and the farm buildings and the sisters' cottage.

They were very able to notice, though, when each of the posts holding the electric fence that was keeping them prisoner did its own small dance and then toppled onto the ground.

Brian and the others started to wonder if they could escape. "We can! We can!" shouted Guinevere Llama.

But the fence had been very tall and now that it was lying down it was very wide. It was, in fact, a big, wide strip of wires, each one full of snaky, bitey electricity, hissing and buzzing in the grass. And if that wasn't enough of a problem, they could hear feet running towards them...

Up over the brow of the hill came a strange sight: the top and then the rest of Badger Bill. "What a very tall badger," said Guinevere.

But then, as Uncle Shawn appeared carrying Bill on his shoulders, the llamas started to be afraid. They weren't sure who was going to make them into pies and shoes and maybe a very tall man and a very short badger would be the ones to do the slish-slashing.

Bill was already afraid enough for several much taller badgers. He knew that the McGloones weren't that far behind and that they were incredibly angry – even for McGloones. And he could hear something else – a noise that made his fur prickle. "What's that sound, Uncle Shawn?"

"Oh, that – that's the electricity in the fence. It's rushing back and forth and waiting to electrocute anyone who comes near it so that they're turned all crispy like toast." Uncle Shawn grinned, as if this wasn't scary.

Bill thought this was scary. Very. "What?!?!?!?!"

Uncle Shawn didn't stop running, but he did slow down a bit so that he didn't scare the llamas by rushing towards them too much. "Oh, yes.

This is the part of my plan that I didn't quite have time to finish..."

"What??!!!???!!!! I don't want to be toast. I've only just escaped being eaten by three dogs."

THINGS BILL DOES NOT WANT TO BE

① A FIGHTER   ② TOAST

③ A PIE   ④ DEAD

JIGGLING

Bill smoothed his ears and patted his whiskers and wrung his paws. "And who are these llamas?" Bill's voice sounded all joggly because Uncle Shawn's running was jiggling him.

"We're going to rescue them. I rescued you and now we rescue them."

"Without a plan?" joggled Bill.

"Without much of a plan…"

The llamas had trotted very nervously towards the fence. Bill

148

saw the eight frightened llama eyes watching him and watching the electrical wires as they writhed and complained like annoyed spaghetti.

"Who are you?" asked Brian Llama, sounding very suspicious and angry. "Because if you've come to slish-slash and make us into wallets and pies, I warn you – we will spit and bite and do terrible things to you." But by the time he'd finished saying this his voice sounded all wobbly and sad and it looked as if he was crying. "Oh, dear," he sighed. The other llamas shook their heads slowly and blinked as they and Bill and Uncle Shawn worked their way along what used to be the fence – lots of bitey electricity humming and fizzing between them.

"We used to be the finest llamas in all Peru," said Guinevere.

"Don't worry," called Uncle Shawn.

"Don't worry?!" complained Bill. "We could be toast at any moment and the McGloones are

coming and they want to make all of us into ...
into ... just one big pie probably."

"Pie!" All the llamas squealed and ran to the
other side of the field and then – "McGloones!" –
they ran back, just as the McGloones did indeed
appear, red-faced and angrier than a washing
machine full of hornets. The fence sizzled, the llamas shuddered and – above all the din – everyone
could hear Maude screeching, "We'll have their
eyessss! We'll have them ssssstewed in butter!"
And her hissing and spitting landed on the fence

and made it crackle. The McGloones started to run round the field to reach Uncle Shawn and Bill who were, by now, the two people they hated most in the world – which is saying something.

"Now, llamas! All is well," called Uncle Shawn, his long legs starting to race again. "My friends the moles have burrowed away underneath the fence and made it fall, but now I need you to be brave and jump over it so that you can come away with me."

The llamas stared at him and stopped trying to keep up. They just stood, looking scared and little.

"There's no time to be scared now. You have to be brave very fast," said Uncle Shawn, glancing at the pursuing horde of McGloones. "Within the next minute or so … maybe less." He was now going clockwise round the remains of the fence and had reached about where six o'clock would be if the big, round, fallen fence had been a clock face. The McGloones were at midnight and were also running clockwise round the fence, trying to get closer. "Please, llamas!"

But the llamas just looked at him. They were so used to being sad and defeated that they couldn't think what they should do.

"Come on!" Uncle Shawn yelled loudly, so that the chasing and scrambling McGloones could hear him. "The dreadful McGloones are here and you know how bad they smell and sound and how dreadful Myrtle is – the only woman horribler than Myrtle is Maude. I mean, they're all TERRIBLE..."

Bill looked over his shoulder at the red-faced McGloones, who had got as far as three o'clock. This was all right, because Uncle Shawn had now run as far as eight o'clock ... but they were getting closer. Bill whispered to Uncle Shawn, "The McGloones are already so angry they look as if their ears will catch fire. Is it wise to make them even angrier by insulting them? Maybe if we said nice things about them…" And Bill tried to think of a compliment to shout at Maude or Ethel, but all he could think of was, "Your voice would scratch windows," which wasn't a compliment at all.

"Please now, llamas," begged Uncle Shawn, "jump! Before you have to look at Bettina McGloone's cardigan. It'll make you sick. And her face… It'll make your fur change colour."

THE CHASE

Meanwhile, the McGloones panted and struggled closer. They had run a long way round and round the fence and they weren't very fit and it was very muddy, which was making it hard to keep going – but still they had reached eight o'clock. And Uncle Shawn was only at where ten o'clock would have been, if they had been running round a nice, safe, big clock instead of a muddy, scary, deadly fence at the top of a round, wet hill.

The llamas stayed still and snuffled and shuffled their hooves. Brian Llama licked his sore hoof. It wasn't really sore, but he always licked it when he was upset.

It didn't help that Fred McGloone (who never usually said anything ever) then screamed at everyone, but mainly Uncle Shawn, "I will suck the marrow from your bones and then make them into whistles, you lanky, smiley, nasty… YOU KNOCKED DOWN OUR HOUSE. IT HAD OUR MONEY IN IT AND OUR KNIVES AND

STICKS AND STONES AND
CHAINS. REVENGE!" It was
the most Fred had ever said and
he was getting nearer, at the
head of all the McGloones.

The smaller McGloones
travelled fastest.

Uncle Shawn just laughed
and shouted back, "I can't hear
you – your face is making me deaf!" Which was a
very rude thing to say, even to a McGloone.

Bill decided he should talk to the llamas, because
he knew how horrible it was to be stuck somewhere
you didn't want to be and to have lost hope. He
tried to keep his voice as unjoggly as possible as he
bounced about on top of Uncle Shawn's shoulders
while they sprinted along. He yelled to the llamas,
"I know you're scared. I'd be scared, too. But Uncle
Shawn is a... He's my friend. He's my first friend...
He's my best friend... And you could come and..."

"And you can stay with us," suggested Uncle Shawn, as if this was a very good and sensible idea. He reached up to his shoulders and patted Bill's paw. "You can all stay with me. We'll have fun."

"Really?" whispered Bill.

"Really," whispered Uncle Shawn. "We just need to get the McGloones annoyed enough and then we can do the rescuing thing. Keep going. You're saying just the right words in just the right order."

"I'm not sure I am."

"I'm sure enough for both of us," said Uncle Shawn.

And so Bill kept talking as Uncle Shawn ran along the outside of the fence and the mud got more trampled and the electricity, it seemed, got more annoyed. But it wasn't as furious as the McGloones.

The McGloones were passing four o'clock now and Uncle Shawn was only just about at five … which wasn't far enough away…

"Come and stay with us, llamas, and we'll have fun together. And … and…" Bill was very scared and the fence was hissing and steaming in the grass like four hundred hot snakes… "We'll have lemonade."

Brian growled, "We've been promised lemonade before."

"No, truly. Uncle Shawn has the best lemonade. Please jump."

WHAT LLAMAS REALLY WANT

LEMONADE

HAMMOCKS

SUNSHINE

¡HOLA!

PORRIDGE
WITH BANANAS
AND STRAWBERRIES

PEOPLE TO SPEAK
TO THEM
IN SPANISH

And close, close, closer was the nasty noise of McGloones running and shouting at each other. "Get out of my way, stoat brains!"

"I'll ssskin those llamasss mysssself. I need a new handbag!" hissed Maude.

And Bill thought he heard the clunking sound of llama knives banging together. "Oh, do jump," he called.

And then there were knives being thrown at him and Uncle Shawn and landing in the grass all around.

"Please, llamas," called Bill.

The McGloones' aim was getting better and better.

"Just be a little bit brave."

The knives were getting nearer.

"We're not brave," said the llamas.

"Of course you are – you stayed in this horrible wet field for ages and didn't get enough to eat and thought you were alone and that you were going to be made into pies – and you put up with all of it. You're the bravest llamas I've met." Actually Bill had never met any other llamas, but he didn't mention that. "JUMP!"

And an especially well-aimed knife whisked clean over the top of Bill's head and gave him a new parting.

"PLEASE!"

And finally Guinevere Llama did jump and just cleared the fence, which crackled as she passed over and singed her ankle fur a tiny bit.

Jump 1

Guinevere

Fence Cleared

singed ankle

Then she and Uncle Shawn had to keep running as the McGloones lunged at them. Socket Wrench McGloone went sliding under Uncle Shawn's left foot, which he'd lifted just in time. The boy went slithering past down the muddy slope, saying bad words as he went.

Then Carlos Llama jumped and was free and he immediately had to dodge Small McGloone and Bettina McGloone as they tried to grab him.

They were again defeated by the mud, which caught at their big, heavy McGloone boots and slowed them. It was getting stickier and oozier the more Uncle Shawn jumped and sprang and ran and danced in it, round and round the field.

And then Ginalolobrigida Llama leapt very

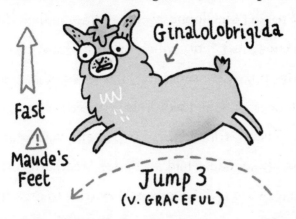

gracefully and landed – not on purpose – right on Maude's feet, squishing her bare toes and making her sit down hugging both her feet and looking like a pile of evil washing. The other McGloones tumbled over her and were now sloshing about in the mud, rolling and biting each other. But it wouldn't be long before they were up on their feet again and galloping round the field in the big broad track of mud their chasing and Uncle Shawn's racing had created.

"Please, please, please," coaxed Bill, still

joggling on Uncle Shawn's shoulder. "What's your name, last llama? And why won't you jump?"

Brian Llama paused and said very quietly, "I'm Brian Llama." And then he asked, "Is it really safe? I don't think it is. I don't think I can jump. I can't." While Bettina McGloone and Socket Wrench McGloone helped each other up and then helped Small McGloone, Brian whispered, "I'm much more scared than the other llamas."

And then – because the McGloones were all back on their feet and so near and so furious, everyone yelled, "BRIAN, YOU'RE THE BRAVEST, MOST FEARLESS AND MAGNIFICENT LLAMA WE'VE EVER MET!"

The McGloones' hands were reaching out and their teeth were grinding.

"Blooming llamas!"

"Chop their ears off!"

"I'll have a chocolate-and-cream-coloured handbag from them if it's the last thing I do!"

And Bill could smell how angry and rotten the McGloones were and he shouted to Brian Llama, "Come on and jump!"

And Uncle Shawn and Carlos and Ginalolobrigida and Guinevere were all dodging and leaping in the mud to avoid McGloone hands that were trying to grab and McGloone feet that were trying to kick them and McGloone mouths that were trying to bite them. It looked as if they were all dancing for their lives, round and round the outside of the fence. Which they were.

And Uncle Shawn shouted to the McGloones, "Are you sure you want to do this? Are you absolutely sure? Do you really want to be so very, very angry?"

And Farmer McGloone yelled back, "We're not nearly as angry as we'll get!" And his head began to swell with fury as if it might burst.

And Maude McGloone screamed, "I'll ssscoop out your insssidesss like iccce cream!" She pointed at Uncle Shawn. "And I'll use your ssskin to make a sssatchel!" Which soaked everyone, including Uncle Shawn, who just shook his head – maybe because he was sad for her and maybe because he was trying to get spit out of his eyebrows.

And then he had to dodge another nearly successful grab at his throat from Myrtle McGloone, who jumped up at him as if she was on nasty, angry springs. Uncle Shawn called to Brian, "Now or never, young llama. You have to jump!"

"Oh, just go on without me," sniffled Brian.

"WE CAN'T!" shouted everyone together, sliding and twisting and hopping round the muddy track they were making muddier by the minute. "YOU'RE OUR FRIEND!"

Uncle Shawn yelled in his loudest yell, "YOU ARE A VERY BRAVE LLAMA! NOW COME HERE SO WE CAN HAVE LEMONADE AND FUN!"

And finally Brian Llama did jump.

And he was sad and tired and scared so his jump wasn't very high.

Not very high

Brian
(SAD AND TIRED)

Slow

Jump 4

And everyone watched as it happened – even the McGloones.

And it seemed that he couldn't make it.

And his whole llama face was really scared, but brave, too.

And then, one-two-three-four, each one of his hooves just managed to miss the fence and carry him to freedom.

And this made Bill and Uncle Shawn and all the other llamas cheer more loudly than they ever had, or thought they could.

And this made Mrs McGloone and Farmer McGloone so completely furious that their ears really did catch light and then they just burst – *POP POP* – like two extremely horrible balloons that you would never want at a party.

It was remarkable.

And this made the other McGloones so angry that they used up the very last of their strength in chasing the llamas and Uncle Shawn (who was

still carrying Badger Bill) as they took off round the fence again.

"Fast as you can!" called Uncle Shawn. "Faster than you have in your lives! Run! I have a plan!"

And so everyone took off in a splatter and scatter of mud, pursued by the remaining McGloones, even the limping Maude.

And when he was right at the top of the field again – at midnight – and the McGloones were right at the bottom – at six o'clock – Uncle Shawn stopped. And then he asked everyone to make the rudest, most annoying faces they could at the McGloones. And he said that they should shout the most insulting insults they could think of.

RUDE AND ANNOYING FACES

And this was very easy for everyone. "Slap feet! Barnacle brains! Lily-livered long-toothed layabouts!" They also said much worse things than that.

And Ethel McGloone and Maude McGloone and Socket Wrench and Small and Bettina and Dusty and Fred McGloone heard the much worse things and then they all took one look at the llamas blowing raspberries and sticking their tongues out at them and Badger Bill crossing his eyes and Uncle Shawn pointing and laughing and wriggling his hair … and they made a terrible mistake.

Each McGloone was too furious to be sensible (and they had all been quite stupid in the first place) and so they decided that the quickest way to get hold of the llamas and Bill and Uncle Shawn would be by taking a shortcut across the field…

And that meant they would take a shortcut across the fence…

They forgot about the fence.

They forgot about the terrible electricity waiting inside the fence to sizzle whoever stepped on it. And their big, heavy, muddy boots and their big, heavy bare feet all stomped down at once with a huge furious *BANG*.

And as soon as they stomped on the sneaky snaky wires, they were turned into toast. They were frizzled and fried and electrocuted into toast, with a fizzing noise and a puff of greasy smoke.

There was a smell of bad pies and then nothing but silence as the wires lost all their electricity and went to sleep.

And the shapes of what used to be McGloones were there in crispy bits of toast dust on the wet grass.

And then the birds began singing and a gentle breeze whiffled past.

And then there was the sound of four llamas and one badger and one uncle being out of breath.

"Well," said Uncle Shawn. "It is always very sad when someone is turned into toast ... but they really did deserve it. They really did." He nodded and sniffed and set down Badger Bill so that he could walk if he wanted, because there was no rush now. "I think that if we go this way, we will meet Paul with my caravan and we can have breakfast and lunch together, both at the same time because we deserve it. You'll like Paul – he is very clever. He's had lessons in seeing in the dark and staring at clouds and listening to vegetables and all the important subjects."

"Are those important subjects?" asked Bill.

"Naturally," said Uncle Shawn.

ALL THE IMPORTANT SUBJECTS

SEEING IN THE DARK

staring at clouds

LISTENING TO VEGETABLES

Bill reached up to take Uncle Shawn's hand, because they were best friends. And together with the llamas they turned their backs on the place where they had not been happy and set off towards somewhere that they would. 🐾

RUBBLE

SECTION EIGHTEEN

In which there are a number of happy endings, because everybody deserves at least one. And as much cake as they would like, because it is a special occasion.

By the following day, a small shower of warm, gentle rain had washed away the McGloone toast shapes. There was only a green hillside with some brown stains in its grass and a broken fence that had lost all its electricity and already started to rust. And where there had been unhappy farm buildings and sad pathways, there were only hollows and heaps of rubble.

In a few years, people who passed near what had

been McGloone Farm would only see some small hills and acres of bushes and trees and wildflowers and meadows, where a large family of goats had decided to live and run a little laundry business, beating the washing on rocks in the stream beside the hollow which had once been the old stables.

Nobody would miss McGloone's Luxury Llama Wool Socks because they made your feet feel sad and nobody likes to have sad feet.

And where there had once been the sign for McGloone Farm, Uncle Shawn had taken away lots of the words so that it read:

STAY HAPPY

PLEASE

A LLAMA'S HEART

Which everybody who passed by thought was very sensible.

And Uncle Shawn and Badger Bill and Paul and the llamas all travelled north after a monstrously

huge lunch and breakfast of jelly and sandwiches and porridge and bananas and earthworms and lemon cake and hay and mint leaves and soup and custard and biscuits and jam roll. Paul pulled the caravan, Bill and Uncle Shawn sitting in it and the llamas trotting alongside, until they wanted a rest and climbed aboard and had their poor patchy coats brushed and their ears tickled by Bill, who thought he was going to like being with llamas.

Soon it was the afternoon and everyone felt much better than they had in ages. They sang songs they made up as they went along:

"Clouds in the sky see us all passing by
And they wiggle their edges
and look at the hedges
And we are all free and very happee."

"Where do you live?" asked Bill as he jiggled next to Uncle Shawn on the driver's seat of the caravan. He was eating an apple because he was still hungry. He was comfortable in his own badger fur and nothing else, and he had rolled in nice clean dust and brushed himself all over, lots and lots, until he had got rid of any McGloone scents that were left on him. He couldn't stop smiling, which made his whole snout a bit different in a good way.

Uncle Shawn said, "Many years ago – before I was born – my great-great-grandfather wrote in his will that his great-great-grandson should inherit a llama farm in a small bay on the sunshiny side of the country." Uncle Shawn tousled his hair with his fingers and his hair tousled them back. "And I never enjoyed having the farm, because I was there all by myself and had no llamas and no best friend to help me…"

Badger Bill's heart got all excited about the idea of a llama farm and he listened with both ears and all his attention.

Uncle Shawn grinned. "So if you would like, William J. Badger, you can live there with me." He called to the llamas, "Would you like to stay with me somewhere on the sunshiny side of the country? In a llama farm with llama barns and llama hammocks and lemonade troughs? I honestly

didn't know what I was going to do with it all until we had our adventure and you rescued me…"

"But you rescued us," said Brian Llama.

"That's how it works," said Uncle Shawn. "You never rescue anyone without getting rescued back."

And the llamas were very happy, if slightly tired. They had been drinking lots and lots of Uncle Shawn's excellent lemonade and eating sweet grass and too much jam roll. Guinevere had hiccups.

"Yes, I'd like it," said Carlos Llama. "But Brian should decide." The llamas turned to smile at Brian and he blushed under what was left of his fur and thought about licking his worry hoof.

"I'd like it, too," said Brian. "I would, a lot. I would like to be with my friends there."

So the llamas cheered and Uncle Shawn and Bill cheered and Paul snorted and huffed, "Well, I'm glad that's sorted out, because I have to be in Aberdeen on Monday. Some of us have busy lives, you know. Then I have to go back to my home in Welsh Wales. Send me a letter when you want the caravan again. And I'll need more warning next time."

And everyone cheered again, so that Paul would smile a little bit – he had lots of big, horsey teeth that it was enjoyable to see. Then they trotted on until they reached the small bay, way up in the north of Scotland on the sun-shiny side of the country.

THE FINE-LOOKING FARMHOUSE

SEA BREEZE

VERANDA

Possibly the finest llama farm in the world

As they came down the soft, sandy path which was perfect for walking on with bare feet or tired hooves, they could see a fine-looking farmhouse. There was a veranda in front of it and some sturdy barns and green fields of rich grass, and the sea breeze made all of them feel very happy, but also very sleepy.

So they unpacked the caravan and had tea and just a little bit of trifle and some small cakes and a pot or two of jam. Then they waved goodbye to Paul and then they explored.

The llamas found that all of the barns were clean and cosy and had good llama hammocks, but the one with the view of the sunset was the best, so they picked that one to live in. Then they nibbled some grass and drank some lemonade out of the trough that Bill filled for them.

"Well done for being brave, Brian," said Guinevere Llama.

"Well done for helping me to be brave," said Brian.

And then all the llamas, snug and dry and warm and happy, went to sleep in their hammocks, snoring in Peruvian accents and with their hooves waving in the air. 🐾

BREAD AND JAM

hot chocolate

SECTION NINETEEN

In which friends get to be friends.

A little later, Badger Bill and Uncle Shawn walked up to the farmhouse holding hands and Bill noticed that there was a badger rocking chair on the veranda, just as if he'd been expected. "Thank you, Uncle Shawn. It's exactly like my own. I think you knew about the McGloones, didn't you? And the poor llamas. You came to get us and take us home. You always had a plan."

"Well," said Uncle Shawn, proudly, "I don't know ... I think I was just ready. And then there were the sad llamas and the bad farmers... And you. And I thought I might perhaps need an adventure and to do some amazing things and to meet some amazing llamas and then maybe find a best friend. And it could be that I'd always thought my best friend might need a rocking chair when I finally found him... Maybe... That could have been my plan all along..." And he winked. "If I'd had a plan..." He grinned an extremely happy grin. "Go and see what the farmhouse is like inside. Your room is upstairs on the left."

BADGER ROCKING CHAIR

Badger Bill scampered off to see how lovely the place would be.

Inside the farmhouse the walls were covered in jam fingerprints and there was butter on the chairs and a lizard reading comics under the sofa, and Bill thought, "Dear me, I'll have to give this a good clean tomorrow." He was a very neat badger.

But once he'd climbed up the stairs with marmalade on the carpet, his own room was as shiny and neat as a new pin. It was painted blue, which was Bill's favourite colour, and it had a snug badger bed with a quilt that had pictures of famous badgers on it. He bounced on the bed and wriggled and jiggled to test that it was comfortable. It was perfect.

(This was either to do with magic, or because Uncle Shawn had guessed the things Bill would like and had sent messages on ahead – carefully remembered and then recited by ravens – and had asked the grown-up squirrels to arrange things…)

Then Bill came downstairs and made some bread and jam and hot chocolate. Next he walked outside on to the veranda where Uncle Shawn was standing and offered him one of the two pieces of bread and one of the two mugs of hot chocolate.

"Hello, Uncle Shawn. I found these mugs in the piano."

"Of course you did." Uncle Shawn smiled and started to drink his chocolate. "This is very good." And to eat his bread and jam. "And this is very good, too."

And then Uncle Shawn sat on the veranda next to Bill, who was in his little badger rocking chair, and they both finished their bread and their chocolate. Then they watched the sun setting and told each other jokes.

"How does a pig go to hospital, Uncle Shawn?"

"In a hambulance, Bill. What do you do if you find a bear in your bed?"

"Get another bed!"

And both of them laughed and Uncle Shawn looked at Badger Bill and thought, "I have a best friend."

And Badger Bill looked at Uncle Shawn and thought exactly the same thing.

They were as happy as happy could be and then a little happier than that. 🐾

AS HAPPY AS
HAPPY COULD BE*

*AND THEN A
LITTLE HAPPIER
THAN THAT

UNCLE SHAWN
AND BILL'S
FAVOURITE JOKES

What's 20 feet
tall and yellow?
A giraffodil.

What's black
and white and goes
up and down ?
*Badger Bill
hopping.*

What's black and white,
over and over?
*Badger Bill doing
somersaults.*

What's black and white and can't climb trees?
*Not Badger Bill because he's very good at climbing
trees, even though he has quite short legs.*

What's very tall
and wavy?
A tree in the wind?
No.
*A snake standing
on tiptoe?*
No.
*Uncle Shawn
waving?*
Yes!

A. L. KENNEDY

A. L. Kennedy was born in a small Scottish town far too long ago and has written books for adults and children, but mainly adults. Before that she made up stories to amuse herself. It has always surprised her that her job involves doing one of the things she loves most and she's very grateful to be a writer. She has won awards for her books in several countries. She has travelled all over the world and enjoyed it immensely. She plays the banjo badly, but makes up for this by never playing it anywhere near anyone else.

GEMMA CORRELL

Gemma Correll is a cartoonist, writer, illustrator and all-round small person. She is author of *A Pug's Guide to Etiquette* and *Doodling for Dog People*, and the illustrator of *Pig and Pug* by Lynne Berry, *Being a Girl* by Hayley Long and *The Trials of Ruby P. Baxter* (among other things). Her illustrations look like a five year old drew them because she hires one to do all her work for her. She pays him in fudge. His name is Alan.